THE HAWK

The last address Petra had for her friend
Sara was the Palazzo Berini. Only
Count Berini denied all knowledge of
her. So Petra watched him, to see if she
could find proof that he was lying to
her, because with a man like Carlo
Berini, anything was possible . . .

THE HAWK OF VENICE

BY
SALLY WENTWORTH

MILLS & BOON LIMITED
15-16 BROOK'S MEWS
LONDON W1A 1DR

*First published in Great Britain 1985
by Mills & Boon Limited*

© Sally Wentworth 1985

*Australian copyright 1985
Philippine copyright 1985
This edition 1985*

ISBN 0 263 75166 X

*Set in Monophoto Times 10 on 11½ pt.
01–1085 – 56694*

*Made and printed in Great Britain by
Richard Clay (The Chaucer Press) Ltd,
Bungay, Suffolk*

CHAPTER ONE

IT was almost four o'clock in the morning when Sara burst into the bedroom, turning on the overhead light and making no attempt to be quiet.

Petra blinked against the light and automatically reached out for her bedside clock, more asleep than awake. When she saw the time she groaned and pulled the covers over her head to try and go back to sleep, but the noise Sara was making made her surface again and prop herself up on one elbow. 'For heaven's sake don't make so much noise; you'll wake everyone up.'

'So what?' Sara retorted, her voice unnaturally high on a note of excitement. 'I couldn't care less.'

Stifling a huge yawn, Petra pulled herself up into a sitting position and tried to free her mind from the clog of sleep. Slowly she became aware that Sara had pulled her suitcase from under the bed and was filling it by the simple method of taking out drawers of clothes and turning them upside down so that the contents fell into the case. 'What on earth are you doing?'

'What does it look like? I'm packing. I'm leaving.' She danced rather than walked the few steps across to the wardrobe, yanking open the doors and starting to pull out clothes. 'I've had as much as I can stand of the Charron family, of being an au pair, and of never having any money.'

'But you can't just leave!' Petra exclaimed, fully awake at last.

'No? Just watch me.' Sara folded some dresses haphazardly and dropped them into the case.

5

'But it's four o'clock in the morning.' Getting out of bed, Petra caught hold of her friend's arm. 'Look, just stand still for a minute, will you, and tell me what this is all about?'

'I've already told you; I've had it up to here with being an au pair. Let's face it, we're nothing better than badly paid drudges. Worse, even, because they make us work all hours and even the kids order us about. Well, I've had it; I'm getting out.'

Petra looked at the other girl in dismay: they had been friends for a great many years and she recognised that implacable note of obstinacy in Sara's voice. But even so, she tried to reason with her. 'Look, I know it's no fun, but at least we're learning the language which is what we came for. And we did say we'd stick it for six months . . .'

'No.' Sara swung away from her and Petra caught the whiff of alcohol on her breath.

'You've been drinking?'

'I have indeed. Champagne no less. And lots of it.' She began to take more clothes from the wardrobe and throw them into her case.

'Hey, that's mine.' Petra tried to take back an evening jacket covered in rainbow-coloured sequins that fractured into a thousand spectrums in the light, but Sara snatched it back.

'Please let me borrow it. I need it. It's the only decent evening jacket we have between us.'

'Why do you need it?' Petra asked, looking at her with some misgivings.

'To wear of course.'

'Why? Where are you going? What's happened to make you suddenly decide to leave?'

'I told you, I'm just fed up with this whole thing.'

'But you can't just walk out in the middle of the night

with nowhere to go . . .' Petra's voice trailed off as she looked at Sara's flushed face closely. 'But you have got somewhere to go, haven't you? You've met someone.' She sighed exasperatedly. 'Oh God, Sara, don't you ever learn? Surely enough men have let you down in the past to . . .'

Sara snapped her fingers. 'To hell with the past! This is the present. And this man isn't like any of the others.' She caught hold of Petra's hands. 'For a start he's rich. *And* he's really something. Dark and with that smouldering Latin look. *You* know what I mean; the type who can undress you with his eyes but make you feel like the most beautiful woman on earth at the same time.' Her eyes glazed a little as she sighed at the pictures conjured up in her own imagination, but then she gave an excited laugh and hurried to put the last of her things into the case.

'But when did you meet him?'

'Tonight. He picked me up in a bar in the Champs Elysées and insisted on taking me to Maxim's. I had a wonderful time, the best I've had since we came to work in Paris.'

'I thought you went out with Jean-Paul tonight?'

'Well, I did start out with him. But, honestly Petra, he got to be really boring, so when I saw Carlo giving me the high sign I decided to go with him instead.'

'Carlo? That doesn't sound very French.'

'It isn't. He's Italian—a Venetian to be exact. And that's where I'm going,' she added gleefully, 'to stay in his Palazzo, no less. The Palazzo Berini. Oh, this is it. I just know it is. He's the kind of man I've been looking for all my life. Rich, handsome and so—so . . .' She sought for a word to describe him. 'So smouldering. He just swept me off my feet.'

'Most of the men you meet seem to sweep you off

your feet,' Petra pointed out sardonically. 'In fact you seem to spend more time up in the air than on the ground. Unless they knock you flat on your back, that is.'

But her sarcasm was wasted on Sara who sat on her case to try and shut it. 'Do the locks up for me, will you? And stop looking so cross. When I marry Carlo I'll invite you to be a bridesmaid and I'll stand you the most wonderful holiday in Venice you've ever known,' she wheedled.

'Huh!' But Petra did as Sara asked, then straightened up and made a last try to make her friend see sense. 'Look, you can't just go off with him now, at this time of night. There won't be any trains. Wait until the morning and . . .'

'But we're not going by train,' Sara interrupted triumphantly. 'Look out of the window. He's waiting for me outside—in that sports car. A blood-red Ferrari no less.'

Going to the window, Petra drew the curtain back and looked down into the parking area in front of the block of flats. The car was there all right, low-slung and gleaming in the lamplight. And there was a dark-haired man standing by it, waiting, his hands up to his face to guard the flame of a lighter as he lit a cigarette. Turning in dismay, she saw that Sara was already at the door, a brilliant, exhilarated smile on her face.

'We're going to drive through the night. It's going to be wonderful; I just know it is.'

'Sara, be careful.' Petra started towards her.

'I will. Don't worry. I'll phone you from Venice.'

'Tell me again where you're staying.'

'The Palazzo Berini.' Sara came back into the room and gave her a quick hug. 'Don't look so worried. Just think of Madame Charron's face in the morning.' Then she gave a crow of laughter and hurried out of the room.

Petra went over to the window again and a few minutes later saw Sara come out of the main entrance to the building. The man, Carlo, threw down his cigarette and took the case from her, putting it into the boot of the car. He had his back to her so Petra couldn't see whether he was handsome or not, but anyway she was on the fifth floor and the lamp wasn't very bright. Sara looked up and waved and the man glanced up briefly but his face was shadowed, then he turned quickly and got into the car, driving out of the car park and accelerating away down the road with the throaty roar of twin exhausts. Slowly Petra drew the curtain and got back into bed, but she lay awake for a long time feeling strangely lonely and wondering just what her friend was heading into this time, and whether she had in fact met the rich Romeo she was always dreaming about.

Sara had been right, Madame Charron's face was a picture the next morning when she found out that Sara had gone. She started a tirade about lazy, unreliable English girls that went on more or less all morning, and insisted on checking every item that was of the least value in the flat to make sure that Sara hadn't taken anything. Petra grimly got on with her work; changing the beds and putting the sheets into the wash, tidying up, cleaning out the two bathrooms, and fumed silently when Madame Charron told her to prepare lunch as well, a job that Sara had always done.

The Charron family were well-to-do by French standards, Monsieur Charron being quite a high-up civil servant. His elderly mother lived with them and there were three little Charrons, two boys and a girl, aged seven, nine and twelve. Petra's own father worked

for UNESCO and when she and Sara had decided to go
to France to study the language he had got them
Charron's name through a colleague who worked in
Paris. Before they had got here it seemed ideal: a luxury
flat in Puteaux on the outskirts of Paris, a respectable
family, and, best of all, work for them in the same place
so that they wouldn't be separated and lonely as they'd
feared. But reality was completely different. The
Charrons paid them only the very minimum legal wage,
often weeks late, and deducted for anything that
Madame Charron decided they'd broken or spoilt; she
even deducted the price of a roast Sara had burnt from
her wages, so that she was left with virtually nothing
one week. Also they were given very little free time to
go to day or evening language study classes as they
were expected not only to baby-sit in the evenings but
to mother-in-law sit when the family went out without
her during the day. And the family as a whole were
pretty ghastly: old Madame Charron expected to be
waited on hand and foot and to have the most personal
things done for her, usually when the girls were in the
middle of doing something else, so that the younger
Madame Charron would start shouting at them and
calling them lazy sluts. Monsieur Charron had made a
pass at each of them in turn, been coldly rebuffed and
now took pleasure in making as much work for them as
possible, and the three children were so used to having
people picking things up after them that it never even
occurred to them to put anything away. They even got
up in the mornings and just stood there, expecting to be
helped to dress.

'Your friend,' Madame Charron shouted. 'She is a
slut, that one. She should never be allowed near my
innocent children. She should have stayed in England
where they have no morals.'

Petra closed her ears to it as much as she could and got on with her work. Life here hadn't been much fun before but it was going to be unbearable without Sara to lighten the days. In fact she was very tempted to follow her example and leave, but in her own way she was as obstinate as Sara and once having made up her mind to do something she kept doggedly on to the bitter end, hating to have to admit defeat. And besides, where could she go? The only other person she knew in Paris was Peter Dudley, her father's friend in UNESCO, who had no room in his crowded household for her to stay. Her own parents were far away in the West Indies, where her father had been sent for a course of duty, their house in England closed up until their return. Petra had some money that she'd brought to France with her, but not enough for a ticket to the West Indies; and she certainly hadn't been able to save any on the Charrons' idea of wages.

The phone rang a couple of times that evening but Petra wasn't surprised when neither of the calls were from Sara; it was a long way from Paris to Venice, something like seven hundred miles, and she expected it to take them a couple of days, especially as they'd started off in the middle of the night after an evening of wining and dining. But after three days, when there had been no call, Petra did start to worry a little, remembering that both Sara and her boyfriend had been drinking which could have led to an accident. Of course Sara wasn't the most reliable of people, especially when in the throes of a new romance, but if she said she'd phone, then she usually kept her word— eventually.

And she did, at seven o'clock the next morning, when Petra was struggling to serve breakfast, get the children ready for school, old Madame Charron was calling her and Monsieur had just had a typically French hand-waving session because she hadn't put the shirt she'd ironed at midnight last night in his room ready for him.

'Oh, Sara, what a time to call. It's bedlam here. Where are you? Still in Venice?'

'Yes, but I'm leaving. Today. And coming back to Paris.'

'Why, what happened? Didn't it work out with Carlo?'

'No,' Sara answered, her voice sounding grim, not like her usual bright self at all. 'Carlo wasn't what he seemed at all. He lied to me all along.'

She went on to say something but the youngest child came up to Petra and demanded that she find his gym shoes while the girl started shouting at her brother, screaming that he'd taken some pencils out of her schoolbag. 'What was that, I didn't hear? Oh, hell. Look Sara, I can't talk now. Are you coming back to work here?'

'No fear. I'll try and find myself another job. I'll come to Paris and phone you again when I get there or else come round to the flat. It should be late tonight or tomorrow morning. If I can't get a job I think I'll go home.'

'All right. See you, then.' Petra put the phone down and was immediately involved in the noisy havoc that was commonplace every weekday morning in the Charron household.

There was little time to think about Sara again until late that evening when Petra had at last finished washing-up after dinner, had finished the rest of the ironing, mended the pockets of one of the boys' blazers that he tore regularly every week, and had collapsed into bed, exhausted. Then she realised that Sara hadn't phoned, but didn't worry; she was bound to get in touch in the morning. But there was no sign of Sara that day or the next, so Petra started to worry all over again.

On the third day she managed to get a couple of hours off and go into the centre of Paris to make enquiries at the language college they were laughingly supposed to attend and among other young people that they'd met since they came to Paris three months ago, but she drew a complete blank. So then she went to the office of their UNESCO friend, Peter Dudley, and asked him if he could find out anything through official channels. This he promised to do but phoned her the next day to say that he, too, couldn't find out anything.

'Look, leave it another couple of days,' he told her. 'And then if Sara hasn't turned up contact me again. Quite honestly no one's going to get very worried about a girl who's gone missing for a few days. Perhaps she changed her mind and decided to tour round Italy while she was there. Or perhaps she got a job. After all, phone calls are expensive, she might have decided to write; there's probably a letter on its way to you in the post.'

'Yes, I expect you're right. Sara always does do things on impulse.'

Petra put the phone down feeling considerably cheered and got on with the task of being a domestic slave to the six laziest people she'd ever known. But when, after nearly a week, there was still no word from Sara, Petra again got in touch with Peter Dudley and this time he checked with the British embassies in France and Italy and also with the police departments in case there had been an accident or something, but again drew a complete blank. Sara hadn't been in touch with any consulate and they had had no word of her. She just seemed to have disappeared completely.

'Don't worry,' Peter Dudley said reassuringly. 'She's probably having such a great time somewhere that she's completely forgotten to phone you.'

But Petra couldn't help worrying; she and Sara had been friends for as long as she could remember and were as close as sisters, closer possibly because there was no jealousy or competition between them. Sara was the flamboyant one, blonde and vivacious, ready to try anything new, meeting people easily and forgetting them just as quickly, whereas Petra was quieter, with chestnut hair framing a serene face with level brows over wide eyes that looked steadily out on the world. High cheekbones, a straight nose and a mouth that always looked as if it was about to break into a smile, added up to a face that wasn't beautiful but held your attention and made you give a second look. Both girls were tall with the slimness of youth and they each acted as foils to the other, Sara impetuous and Petra sensible.

At the end of the week, when there was still no telephone call or letter from Sara, Petra waited until Monsieur and Madame Charron had gone out one evening, the children were safely in bed and the *belle-mère* glued to her favourite television soap-opera, then she sneaked into the study, picked up the phone and asked the operator to give her the number of the Palazzo Berini in Venice. It took quite a long time before she was connected; various operators across the two countries kept coming on the line and telling her to wait, but at last she heard the number ringing and waited, rather nervously, for someone to answer, all the while in her mind rehearsing all the things she would have to say to Sara for not getting in touch, already imagining the angry relief she would feel when she heard her friend's voice.

After what seemed like ages a woman's voice

answered, but it wasn't Sara. This woman was older and spoke in Italian, but Petra made out the words Palazzo Berini.

'Please, do you speak English?' she hazarded, and then into the silence, *'Parlez-vous Français?'*

'Palazzo Berini,' the woman repeated impatiently.

'Could I speak to Miss Sara Hamling, please?'

There was silence at the end of the line and then, to Petra's indignation, the receiver was replaced and she was left with a dead phone.

Her first instinct was to dial again immediately, but a couple of seconds' thought made Petra realise that it would be a waste of time, she would only get the same woman again, who obviously didn't understand a word she was saying.

It was the early afternoon of the next day before Petra was able to phone again. To her annoyance the same woman answered but this time Petra changed her tactics. 'Carlo Berini, *per favore.'*

The woman said something that sounded like Count Berini and some other words Petra didn't understand, then there was the sound of the receiver being set down and a long silence before it was picked up again and a man's voice answered. *'Pronto.'*

'Hallo. Er—is that Carlo Berini?'

'Yes, I am Count Berini.' The voice was short, authoritative, speaking in fluent English with hardly any trace of an accent.

'My name is Petra Thornton. We haven't met, but I'm a friend of Sara's.'

'Sara's. Sara who?'

'Sara Hamling, of course.'

There was a few seconds of silence before Carlo Berini said, his voice heavily sardonic, 'I don't know who you're talking about, I know no one of that name.'

'But you do,' Petra protested. 'You took Sara to Venice with you two weeks ago to stay at your Palazzo. You met her in Paris. You must remember.'

His voice grew annoyed. 'Either you have got the wrong number or this is some kind of joke. In either case I do not intend to pursue this conversation any further.'

'No, wait,' Petra cried out, in a panic in case he put down the receiver. 'The person I want is called Carlo Berini and lives at the Palazzo Berini in Venice. Is that you?'

'That is most definitely I.'

'And there's no other Carlo Berini?'

'No. I am the only man to bear that name,' he told her haughtily.

'Then you *must* know Sara.'

'As I said before, you are mistaken. I do not know your friend and she has certainly never stayed in this house,' he replied shortly. Petra tried to protest but his voice overrode hers, 'I suggest you look for your friend elsewhere. And do not call this number again.'

Then he replaced the receiver, cutting off Petra's protesting voice. She stood there for several minutes, trying to work it out. Why on earth had this Carlo Berini denied all knowledge of Sara? Unless he was ashamed of having picked her up. Or that woman who'd answered the phone—could she be his wife? And if she'd been nearby, listening, then he would have had to deny Sara having been there. When she'd phoned, Sara had said that he'd lied to her; perhaps that was why, because he was married. But it didn't help her to find Sara. Petra sat down in Madame Charron's favourite armchair and tried to work out what to do. She supposed she could try phoning Count Berini again in the hope of catching him when his wife wasn't around, when he might tell her the truth, but the woman had answered both times and might get suspicious if Petra kept calling, in which case the Count could get angry and refuse to tell her anything. If he could deliberately lie to a girl to get her to go away with him, then he was quite capable of going on with his pretence of not knowing anything about Sara. Once a swine always a swine!

Petra was so deep in thought that she didn't hear Madame Charron come into the flat and her employer immediately went into a Gallic tantrum when she found her sitting down instead of working. 'You lazy girl. Why are you not cleaning out the bedrooms as I told you to? And you still have all the shoes to clean and the shopping to do yet. Do you think I pay you to sit around and do nothing?'

Her first feeling had been of guilt and Petra had jumped quickly to her feet, but the unfairness of the accusation suddenly got to her and she faced up to the irate Frenchwoman. 'You hardly pay me at all. You haven't given me any wages for the past five weeks, and you owe Sara three weeks' money.' She held out her hand and said determinedly, 'I'd like it now, please.'

Madame Charron looked taken aback and began to bluster. 'I will pay you on Saturday, *comme d'habitude*. Now get on with your work.'

But Petra stood her ground. 'No, I want it now.'

'Do you think I have that much money in the house? You will have to wait.'

Petra sat back in the chair. 'All right, I'll wait here.'

'You insolent girl! How dare you? If you don't get up at once I will telephone my husband.'

'Good, maybe he'll have some money,' Petra retorted, folding her arms and prepared to sit it out as long as necessary.

'You English!' Madame Charron gestured eloquently.
'All you think about is money, money. Always going on
strike. No wonder your country is ruined, *fini*.' Then,
finding that she was having no effect, 'I can let you
have two weeks' money, but that is all I have.'

'All of it,' Petra answered shortly, knowing full well
that Madame Charron always had plenty of money in
her purse for shopping, petrol, etc. She certainly never
went short of anything she wanted.

After a bit more arm waving and verbal abuse, her
employer looked at the clock and realised that if Petra
didn't go and do the shopping now she would be back
late to start the dinner and then her husband would be
annoyed and accuse her of not being able to run the
household, and his mother would add her voice to his.
'Oh, very well, but it means that I will have no money
left to give to the children for their lunches tomorrow.
The poor darlings will have to go hungry because of
you, you ungrateful girl. After all we have done for you,
giving you a home.'

Petra raised her head and looked her silently in the
face and the woman looked discomfited and turned
away to get her bag. 'Here, there is the money for the
last five weeks. Not that you deserve it, you never do
anything properly.'

'And Sara's,' Petra insisted.

'You are going to take her money, too? No, you will
only keep it and spend it on yourself. I will keep it for
her. She can have it when she comes to apologise to me
for walking out like a thief in the night.' But her attitude
changed when Petra sat down in the chair again. 'Oh,
very well. All right. Here is her money. But I want a
receipt for it. Or else she will come back and demand it
of me, I know. Now, go and do the shopping. Quickly,
before the shops close. Here is the list of what I want.'

Taking the list from her, Petra said, 'The money, please.'

'The money! Do you not know I have none left? You must get it out of your wages and I will pay you back on Saturday.' Petra just laughed at her and the woman angrily took a hundred franc note from her purse and thrust it at her. 'Here. And I want bills for every centime you spend. I expect you have both been robbing us whenever you can.'

A flush of resentment and anger came into Petra's face. She was always scrupulous about money and had never in her life taken a penny that wasn't hers. In that moment she decided exactly what she was going to do, about Madame Charron and about Sara. After doing the shopping, she prepared dinner and ate hers in the kitchen after waiting on the family in the dining-room, then she did the washing-up and cleared the kitchen, leaving it scrupulously clean. Only then did she go to her own room, pack all her things and walk out of the flat, catching a bus to take her into central Paris and Austerlitz station where she booked a ticket on the next train to Venice.

While she was waiting for the train, Petra again phoned Peter Dudley to let him know what she was doing. He wasn't at all encouraging. 'I feel you're wasting your time, Petra. Sara could quite well be here in Paris, or she might even have gone home to England.'

'Not without telling me,' Petra replied positively. 'She'd never do that. I'm sure something has happened to her, and the only way I can find out is by going to Venice to try to learn what went wrong there and how she intended to get back to Paris.'

'By train, I should think.'

'Yes, but you know what Sara's like; if someone

offered her a lift she might well take it. Anyway, I have
to get hold of this Count Berini to talk to him.'

'All right, keep me posted. I might hear something
this end. And be careful—okay? The way you young
girls trot around Europe makes my hair stand on end
sometimes.'

Petra laughed; Peter Dudley was completely bald and
hadn't had any hair to stand on end for years. 'I will.
Thanks for what you're doing. I'm sorry to be such a
nuisance.'

'No trouble. 'Bye.'

The train to Venice was a slow one, stopping at every
station along the line, and Petra had bought the
cheapest ticket so had to sit up all night, squashed
between a man who whistled through his teeth when he
slept and a nun who clicked her rosary the whole time.
Once they stopped in a station to change engines and
she looked out of the window to see the revamped
Orient Express drawn up at a nearby platform. It was
brightly lit with ornate shaded lamps in each window
and she could see people standing round a bar and a
grand piano, the women in expensive evening dresses,
the men in dinner jackets and bow ties, laughing and
drinking. Next to the bar was a restaurant car where
late diners sat in space and comfort, waited on by
attentive men in the old-fashioned blue uniforms of the
original Orient Express. As Petra watched one of them
brought a bottle of champagne to a table and she heard
the rich pop it made even in her own crowded carriage.
She licked her lips, feeling thirsty as she watched the
sparkling wine poured into glasses cut to catch the light,
but then the Orient Express pulled out of the station,
leaving an empty platform, and she sat back in her seat
with an envious sigh, having seen for a moment how the
other half live.

She got to Venice at about eight the next morning, feeling tired and untidy, but as Petra came out of the station, down the wide steps, and saw the Grand Canal spread out before her, bright in the morning sun, everything else was forgotten. It was like a different world, the boats on the canal and the gondolas tied up on the opposite bank, an ornate bridge to her left and an old, green-domed church across the wide stretch of water. The feeling of Venice was there the minute you came out of the station.

She immediately wanted to begin to explore, to feast her eyes on the beautiful city, but first things first. Ever practical, Petra had checked her case into the left luggage section and had got a street map—or canal map rather—from the tourist office in the station. Now all she had to do was to find the Palazzo Berini. Easier said than done; there were dozens of palaces marked on the map, both bordering the Grand Canal and the lesser canals that weaved their way through the maze of islands that made up the city of Venice. At last she found it, facing the Grand Canal but with another, much smaller canal on one side of the building. It looked a long way on foot but the way to get around here seemed to be by water bus and there was a stop nearby, 'Vaporetto' it said. There had been an Exchange place in the station where Petra had changed her French francs into Italian lire, so she was able to put some money into the ticket machine and then wait for the Linea One boat going down the canal to St Mark's Square.

At this time of the day the canal boats were full of people going to work and Petra was squeezed into a corner, unable to look out of the windows and see the passing scenery. It reminded her vividly of travelling on the London Underground in the rush hour. The boat was continually full as new people took the places of those that got off, but after a few stops Petra was able to stand by the rail where passengers disembarked, her map in her hands, looking out eagerly for the Palazzo Berini. The vaporetto criss-crossed from side to side of the wide canal, hooting imperiously at other boats that got in the way and stopping at wooden jetties that moved with the waves of water from the wash.

A great many of the big palazzi had been turned into hotels and, because they all joined on to one another, it was sometimes difficult to see where one ended and the next began. But as they drew nearer, Petra held on to the rail and craned her head out, counting the number of buildings down from where a river joined the canal: one, two, three, a little street that wasn't much more than an alleyway, four, then, on a corner where blue water showed the entrance to another canal, that must be it!

Petra stared at the large, pastel-coloured building with its delicately carved Gothic tracery columns and windows. It had three storeys, the first with a large, arched central doorway with marble steps down to the water's edge and the blue-and-white spiral painted posts topped with gold birds to which boats could tie up. The second storey had balconies at the windows, and the third, just as high, but the windows were without balconies this time. On either side of the doorway there were stone escutcheons of some sort, but Petra hadn't time to look at them properly before they were past and she was scrambling to get off the boat at the next stop, a little further down the canal.

It was only after she got off that Petra realised that, although the Palazzo was easy enough to find from the canal, finding it on foot was another matter. She had to walk down a wide alleyway which opened into a square with canals on three sides, then turn left, go over a bridge and find another alley that led in the direction of the palazzo. She turned left again, thinking that she'd found the building, but the alley came to a dead end and she had to retrace her steps and go on further. The alley turned sharp right for a short while, but there was another alley leading off left, and she could see the grand canal at the end of it. This had to be the place.

The alley had high walls but on her left she could see that trees grew on the other side, and the alleyway was clean, without any rubbish, as if it was swept every day. Then, further along, there was a door set into the wall, a high, elegant door with the words 'Palazzo Berini' set above the letter-box and an old-fashioned ornate iron bell-pull.

Petra gulped, feeling suddenly nervous now that she had actually found the place. What if this Count Berini wasn't at home and his wife answered the door? What on earth could she say to her? Glancing at her watch, Petra saw that it was half-past nine. If the Count went out to business he would have gone by now. Then again he might be rich enough not to have to go out to work. Entirely ignorant of the ways of the Venetian nobility, Petra was in a quandary. She could hang about at the end of the alley and keep an eye on the side door, but either the Count or his wife could quite easily leave or arrive by boat at the front. And the alley ended at the end of the building which was also the water's edge, so short of standing at the very end and craning dangerously forward to see, there was no way she could watch both doors. And anyone who saw her doing that was likely to feel highly suspicious. She tried it, holding on to the small iron gate that blocked off the alley, the water almost level with her feet, and peered round to the front of the building, but was unable to see the

actual door, only the steps leading up to it and the blue-
and-white barber poles. Now that she was closer Petra
could see that the gold birds on top of them were
hawks, their wings outspread as if to swoop upon their
prey, their beaks sharp enough to tear it apart. She
shivered and walked back the way she'd come.

A rumble in her tummy reminded Petra that she
hadn't had any breakfast so she decided to go and eat
while she thought the matter over. There was a café
with tables outside in the little square near the
vaporetto stop, so Petra sat at one of them in the sun
and ordered coffee and rolls. She bit into them
hungrily, with all the appetite of youth. The waiter
offered to open the gaudy blue-and-white striped
parasol poked into a hole in the middle of her table, but
Petra shook her head, enjoying the sun. Having a day
off like this made her realise just how hard she had been
working for the last three months. If she'd still been at
the Charrons' now she would have been washing up the
breakfast things in between helping old Madame
Charron in and out of her bath and answering the
phone and the door, the bells of which always seemed
to ring whenever she had her hands in water.

But this, this was bliss. Petra ate the last crumb
and drained the last drop of coffee, then leaned back
in her chair, eyes closed against the sun. How lovely
to just sit and relax all day. She sighed and opened
her eyes. This wouldn't do, she still had the problem
of Sara to solve. The waiter came up to her and
smiled, asked her in his broken English if she wanted
anything else. He was young, only about sixteen, and
his eyes travelled over her appreciatively. The sun
must have set her brain working because Petra had an
idea. Smiling back at the waiter, she said, 'No, thank
you. That was delicious—very good,' she amended

when he frowned. 'Do you live in Venice?' Silly question but at least it was an opener.

'*Si.*' He gestured expansively towards the café and upwards. 'I live in this house.' He lifted his hand again. 'Much high.'

'How exciting. You must know Venice well?'

'*Si.* I live here all my life.'

'And the palazzi, I expect you know all about them?'

'But of course,' he boasted, pleased to air his knowledge, 'I know all the palazzi.'

'There are some beautiful ones near here. I especially noticed the one with the lovely windows.' She pretended to consult her map. 'Palazzo Berini, is it called?'

'Ah, *si*. The Palazzo Berini. Is very old. Very beautiful.'

'Oh, yes, it is.' Petra tried to put all the fervour of an ardent tourist into her voice. 'And you know it well? How lucky you are. Have you been inside it?'

His eyes shadowed for a moment as vanity fought with truth, but then he shrugged. 'Inside it, no. It is a private palazzo, you understand? Not open to the public.'

'Oh, what a shame. Who lives there?' she asked, as casually as she could.

'It is the Count Berini. His family has lived there many years, many centuries.'

'Really? How interesting. Do you know, I think I've heard of him. Is he Count Carlo Berini?'

'*Si.* That is his name.'

'And his wife, the countess, what's her name now?'

The waiter shook his head. 'There is no countess. The Count is not yet married and his mother died many years ago.'

So who was the woman who had answered the phone? And the boy had said, 'not yet married'. Did

that mean the Count was engaged or something? Petra
opened her mouth to ask but the boy was looking at her
rather strangely and she decided she'd asked enough
about the Count. So she smiled at him and asked him
about the Rialto Bridge. He launched happily into a
description of its history, enjoying improving his
English, but then another customer called him over. 'I
have to go. But you come again, eh? My name is
Vasco.' He pressed her hand and waved away the
money for her breakfast, but when he'd gone Petra left
it on the table. She might need to question Vasco again
and she didn't want to owe him in any way, he looked
too amorous for that.

Her steps took her back in the direction of the Berini
palace, slowly at first but then Petra quickened her
pace. She was going to beard this playboy in his den,
and if he was engaged and his fiancée found out about
Sara, then it was just too bad. As far as Petra was
concerned, he was the type who deserved everything he
got! Going up to the door, Petra pulled the bell as hard
as she could.

CHAPTER TWO

THE sound of the bell jangled far into the depths of the house, like an echo in a cavern, but it was answered surprisingly quickly. The big, faceless door opened silently and Petra was confronted by a middle-aged woman in a navy blue dress, her dark hair pulled back into an uncompromising bun. Petra guessed at once that this was the maid or housekeeper; after all she was more or less a servant herself, and it takes one to know one, she thought wryly. The woman said something to her in Italian and Petra recognised the voice that had spoken to her on the phone. Why hadn't it occurred to her that it could be a housekeeper?

'Count Berini, *per favore.*'

The woman said something else and Petra shook her head. 'I'm sorry, I don't understand you. *Non parlo italiano.*'

Frowning, the woman said in heavily accented English, 'What is your name?'

'Miss Thornton. I wish to see Count Berini.'

Instead of letting her in, the housekeeper stood hesitating for a long moment and looked as if she was going to refuse, so Petra, in a slight panic, stepped forward and more or less pushed her way in.

'Count Berini,' she insisted.

The woman looked annoyed, but reluctantly stepped back and let Petra come right in. 'You wait here,' she said grudgingly and walked away.

Stepping through the doorway set into the blank outside wall was like stepping into an Aladdin's cave.

27

The floor was of pale pink marble, the walls half panelled and very high, the upper half hung with large paintings, and the ceiling too was beautifully ornate, a mixture of carved wood and painted scenes. Not bad for the back hall, Petra thought, trying hard not to be overpowered by all the grandeur.

After what seemed like an age, the woman came back and motioned Petra to follow her. They walked through into a huge inner hallway, even more beautiful than the first, with large tapestries on the wall, and up a wide marble staircase to the first floor. Petra looked at all the works of art around her and for the first time became conscious of her crumpled blouse and skirt, old ones that were good enough for travelling in, and her dusty feet in just a pair of sandals. She wished suddenly that she'd found somewhere to stay and had had a bath and changed before she came.

She wished it even more when the housekeeper showed her into a salon overlooking the canal and she came face to face with Count Carlo Berini. He was seated at a large and beautifully ornate desk, but looked up as she came in and then got slowly to his feet. He was tall for an Italian, over six feet, and quite slim, but not effetely so, his was the kind of athletic slimness that was all whipcord muscle and caged strength, a body ruled by the mind and not by its appetites. He was dark haired and dark eyed, and there was something indefinably aristocratic about his features, perhaps it was his high cheekbones and straight nose. His mouth was thin but there was something sensual about it, something that drew Petra's eyes and held them. Reluctantly she raised them and found herself being looked over just as candidly by a pair of mocking dark eyes. Her cheeks reddening, Petra drew herself up, remembering why she'd come.

'Good morning,' Count Berini said to her, his voice sounding deeper than it had on the phone. 'You wished to see me, I believe?'

'Yes. My name is Thornton, Petra Thornton, and I . . .'

'Ah yes,' he interrupted before she could finish. 'The young lady who phoned yesterday. About a friend of yours, was it not?'

'Yes. It was about Sara.'

He raised a questioning eyebrow when she didn't go on. 'So?'

'So where is she?' Petra demanded flatly.

Carlo Berini frowned and then sat down again, sitting back in his chair and looking at her over hands tapered into a pyramid. 'I believe I told you at the time that I have never heard of your friend?'

Petra nodded. 'Yes, you did.'

'So why have you come here?'

'Because . . .' What was the use of prevaricating? 'Because I didn't believe you. I *know* Sara came here. With you.'

He leaned forward, his eyes frowning and Petra was suddenly reminded of the symbolic hawks. 'Are you accusing me of lying?' he demanded grimly.

Petra swallowed nervously, but said, 'You should know whether you're lying or not. All I know is that Sara said she was going to Venice with you, and a few days later she phoned to say that . . . to say that things hadn't worked out and she was coming back to Paris. But she never arrived. And that was over a week ago. So I came here to find her, because this is the last place I know that she'd been staying.'

'I see.' He was more relaxed now but his frown had deepened. 'You say that she gave you my name and this address?'

'Yes.' Petra nodded eagerly, waiting for him to go on, but he merely shrugged eloquently.

'Your friend must have made a mistake. I do not know her and I certainly never gave her a lift to Venice.' He stood up and said dismissively, 'I'm sorry I cannot help you but . . .'

'It was more than just a lift,' Petra broke in. 'You picked her up in a nightclub and brought her back here to—to stay with you. If you see what I mean.'

Count Berini did. His nostrils flared distastefully. 'I am not in the habit of picking up girls in nightclubs, Miss Thornton. Nor would I dream of bringing such a person back to this house.'

'But you did; Sara said so.'

'And you would take this girl's word before mine?' he demanded, six hundred years of Venetian nobility in his tone. 'A girl who allows herself to be picked up and goes with men she has only just met?'

Bright spots of colour came into Petra's cheeks, but her chin came up in defence of her friend. 'Yes, I would. Because whatever else she does, Sara never tells lies.'

His mouth drawing into a thin line, Count Berini stated coldly, 'I do not intend to waste my time in repeating what I have already said. I suggest you look for your friend elsewhere. If she can so readily entrust herself to one man then she might just as easily have gone with another.'

Petra shook her head. 'No, the man would have to be pretty special before she'd go with him.' Carlo Berini's left eyebrow rose sardonically and Petra realised that she'd paid him a very one-sided kind of compliment. 'What I mean is, Sara wouldn't go off with just anyone.'

He looked at her sneeringly. 'Your morals and those

of your friends are of no interest to me, Miss Thornton.'

Which made her feel about as low as an alley cat. 'Are you going to tell me where Sara is?' she demanded, her voice rising in anger.

'For the last time; I cannot tell you what I do not know,' he answered exasperatedly.

'Very well. In that case I shall go to the police.'

His eyebrows rose incredulously. 'Are you threatening me, Miss Thornton?'

'Yes, I am,' Petra returned, tossing her head defiantly.

Carlo Berini stared at her disbelievingly for a long moment, then his eyes travelled over her as if he was really looking at her for the first time. 'And do you really think they would believe your story—any more than I do?'

'That I'll find out—because I'm definitely going to them.'

'Then I suggest you do so,' he said softly, reaching out to press a bell on his desk. 'Maria will see you out.'

It was said dismissively and Petra couldn't think of anything more to say before the housekeeper opened the door, so quickly that she must have been waiting almost outside. Petra took one more look at this man, this hawk of Venice, then turned quickly on her heel and marched angrily out of the room.

She was so annoyed with the way she'd been brushed off that it didn't occur to Petra until she was outside in the alley again, the big wooden door closed behind her, that she should have tried to talk to the housekeeper; if Carlo Berini did take girls to the palazzo then his servant was bound to know about it. Petra knew full well from her own relatively short experience as an au pair that there was very little that went on in a household that the hired help didn't know about. She turned, her hand raised to the bell-pull again, but then hesitated, thinking it might be better to get the woman, Maria, on her own before she started asking any questions.

Slowly she turned away wondering what to do next. Her threat to go to the police hadn't been entirely an idle one; if she could find no trace of Sara she would certainly go to them, but her mind boggled at the thought of trying to explain to foreigners, especially when she had no evidence other than what Sara had told her. And now that she had seen Carlo Berini her heart sank even more; he had been right, the Venetian police were hardly likely to take her word against his, a native Venetian and a nobleman at that. If only she could find some proof that Sara had been there. She decided to wait until she had the opportunity to talk to Maria, and in the meantime watch the palazzo as closely as she could.

Her decision made, Petra turned her steps more briskly in the direction of the café where she'd had breakfast. If she was going to keep an eye on the palazzo then it would help to stay somewhere nearby and Vasco seemed the ideal person to ask if he knew anywhere.

He did. He suggested a room on the same floor as his own above the café. 'It is not big, but it is cheap, you understand,' he told her, immediately recognising that she didn't have much money.

Petra was dubious, not sure that she wanted to be that close to Vasco if he decided to make a pass, but he could be very useful in her search for Sara. 'Perhaps I could have a look at the room?' she said.

'*Si*. I fetch Emilio. He is the . . .' he sought for the word and came up with, 'proprietor.'

He went back into the interior of the café and a few minutes later came out with a moustached Italian who looked as if he liked to sample his own food and drink from the size of his stomach. After looking Petra up and down he poured out a spate of Italian, his hands gesturing like mad. Evidently he didn't speak a word of English.

'Emilio is the cousin of my cousin,' Vasco explained, evidently thinking this a close family tie. 'His daughter, Lucia, she has gone to Milan for one month. You can have her room for that time, or—or shorter time, you understand? But Emilio, he says you must not touch her clothes, her things.'

Petra nodded. 'I understand. I'll be very careful.'

Vasco translated for Emilio, who immediately poured out another string of Italian. Vasco flushed a little. 'And Emilio, he says there must be no men, no boyfriends.'

Well, that was a relief, with Emilio to keep an eye on Vasco she should be safe; perhaps he'd got Vasco lined up for his own daughter. Petra nodded gravely at Emilio, trying to impress him with her absolute uninterest in men. He seemed satisfied and Vasco led her into the café, through a door at the back that gave into a big kitchen where a woman was working, and up a steep flight of stairs to the first floor and then up two more, even narrower flights to the top floor. Land was so scarce in Venice that every building had at least three storeys. There were three doors opening off the top landing and Vasco took her to the one on the left, his presumably was one of the others. It was a larger room than Petra had expected, about ten feet square, and looking out over the back of the house into a small courtyard surrounded by the backs of similar buildings. The room was quite pleasant with a single bed, an old-fashioned handbasin in one corner and wallpaper with big, garish flowers in faded shades of deep pink and mauve. The only ornate feature was a glass chandelier, typical of Venice, with flowers, chains and droplets in confusing abundance, and it hung so low that you had to walk round it or else knock into it and set all the glass tinkling.

'How much is the rent?' Petra asked, although she'd already made up her mind to take the room if she could afford it. Vasco named a sum of several thousand lire, which sounded like a fortune but which, when she laboriously changed it into English money, came down to a very reasonable sum.

'And for that you also get continental breakfast,' Vasco told her, misunderstanding her silence during her mental calculations.

Petra gave him her best smile. 'I'll take it, then. And thank you very much for telling me about it, Vasco.'

He returned her smile with one that would set some female hearts fluttering in a few years, if it hadn't already started to do so. 'Perhaps, in return, you would help me with the English. I wish for a job in the Cipriani or the Gritti Palace,' he told her, naming the two best hotels in Venice. 'But for these hotels you must have the very good English.'

'You want to get a job there as a waiter?'

He looked shocked. 'But no, Signorina, I wish to be . . .' he struggled for the words, 'at the desk, a—a concierge.'

'A receptionist,' Petra supplied. 'Will you tell your cousin that I'll take the room? I left my luggage at the station so I have to go and collect it.'

As they went downstairs she told Vasco her name and he showed her a back way into the café through the courtyard and a tiny alley into a street that ran at right angles to the one on which the café fronted. It was still early so Petra decided to walk to the station, following her map and the yellow-painted direction signs that led her through cobbled alleys of shops with bright but expensive clothes, through small squares dominated by large churches, over little hump-backed bridges that crossed small and rather smelly secondary canals, and on until she came again to the Grand Canal and crossed the graceful stone bridge that led to the station. There was no question of walking back, her suitcase was heavy and it was a difficult enough task to find space for it in the vaporetto; as it was her holdall would have got knocked into the canal if she hadn't managed to grab it from between the legs of a tall tourist who kicked it to one side.

Entering the café by the back way, Petra humped the cases up the narrow staircase, then went over to sit on the window sill to get her breath back and cool off a little. It was hot outside but the sun had moved round now and the room was in shadow. Looking out into the courtyard with its storey upon storey of shuttered windows, Petra decided that the back of Venice was by no means as beautiful as the front. Here the brickwork was exposed and crumbling, the green paint on the shutters peeled and faded almost into non-existence. Washing hung from poles extended from the windows and the red-pantiled roofs were adorned with TV aerials, flue pipes and cement chimneys. On the ground there were several dustbins full of rubbish and a pile of timbers that looked like the remains of a gondola. The only pleasant thing in the courtyard were a canary in a cage fixed to a wall and some plants on a window sill, their red flowers making a bright patch of colour against the peeling grey wall.

Her eyes lifted to where she could just see the roofs of

taller, grander buildings near the canal. Was one of them the roof of the Palazzo Berini? Petra's thoughts flew back to her interview with the owner of all that grandeur. She didn't envy him his palace; it must be like living in a museum. How could you enjoy life when you were always afraid that you might scratch or break something that was priceless? She remembered the way Count Berini had looked at her; with his lean, dark features he wasn't unlike the emblem of a hawk. She shivered a little, realising that she had taken on a tough adversary. If he went on insisting that he knew nothing about Sara, then the only way she could force him into telling the truth was by finding some proof that Sara had been in the palazzo. And she wouldn't find that by sitting in this room. Jumping to her feet, Petra unpacked some of her clothes, careful to touch nothing that belonged to the absent Lucia, then had a stand-up wash and changed into a clean dress. Sitting down at the over-ornate dressing table, she brushed her hair, flicking it up at the edges, and applied a little lipstick, which was usually all the make-up she wore, then went down to the café for a late lunch, feeling far more confident and ready to get down to her search again.

But the rest of that day was almost a complete waste of time. The only place where she could watch the front of the palazzo properly from that side of the canal, was from the jetty of the vaporetto stop that jutted out into the water, but from there it was impossible to see the side door, so Petra had to divide her time between the two places and just hope that she would strike lucky. But there was no sign of any occupant from the palazzo until about eight o'clock that evening when she was sitting on one of the green plastic seats in the waiting area of the vaporetto jetty. Almost, she had given up hope, and she took little notice of a sleek and very powerful-looking motorboat that came up fast from the direction of St Mark's Basin, followed by a much older craft. The speedboat slowed down as it went past and curved gracefully in towards the bank, negotiated the mooring poles and drew up neatly beside the steps of the Palazzo Berini.

Petra was immediately on her feet and pushed past the other people to stand on the edge of the jetty, holding on to the rail and leaning forward to see. The boat was tied up and a man got out, but it wasn't Carlo Berini, then the other, slower boat came up and moored alongside. The man went to the big doors and stood there for some minutes, possibly talking to someone inside, although Petra couldn't see who, then he got into the second boat and it turned and went back the way it had come.

Trying to work it out, Petra decided that the man had merely delivered the boat after it had been repaired or something, and that it must belong to Carlo Berini. It was a beautiful boat of varnished wood and bright chrome with an open cockpit and a small cabin, but she looked at it in dismay. How could she possibly hope to follow him if he went out in that? All the disadvantages of a city whose main street was a stretch of water came home to her. You couldn't just hire a passing taxi and say, 'Follow that boat.' Water taxis were only found at special taxi stations and you had to go to them, not them to you. She watched for another hour in case Count Berini used the boat, but he didn't come out and by then it was growing dark and it was difficult to see. Petra got stiffly to her feet and went to a pizza restaurant where you watched the cook make your pizza and it came to you piping hot and thick with ham and cheese. Then there was nothing to do but to go back to the café and phone Peter Dudley in case Sara had turned up, but there was still no news from that end.

Petra was up very early the next morning to resume her watch on the palazzo, but even so she was almost too late. As she came out of the front of the café she just caught a glimpse of a woman walking by, a big basket on her arm, and was almost sure that it was Maria, the housekeeper. She wasn't completely sure because she'd been too nervous the first time and too angry the second time she'd seen her to take that much notice of the woman's features, but that glance was enough to send her hurrying in the woman's wake.

The narrow lanes were crowded with people all heading in the same direction, mainly housewives with bags or baskets, and Petra guessed there must be some sort of early morning market where they all went to get their groceries. It made it hard to follow the woman, but eventually Petra got close enough to be sure it was Maria and to keep her in sight. Should she stop her and ask about Sara? Petra shrank from doing so in these noisy, narrow streets, where there was nowhere they could stand aside and talk. It would be difficult enough when she didn't speak Italian anyway, although she knew that Maria spoke some English. So she followed the woman to a bridge across the canal which Petra recognised as the Rialto, both sides of which, except for the central section, she was surprised to see lined with small shops in each of the arches. But Maria went across the bridge to a big market on the other side, and Petra watched as she went from one stall to another and bought red and green peppers, fat ripe tomatoes and half a dozen different kinds of olive. Then Maria went in to the roofed enclosure of a fish market where she stood for several minutes haggling over the price of two large red lobsters. It wasn't so crowded in this part of

the market and Petra could see an area just outside
where the fishmongers' barrows were left and where
there weren't any people. Moving forward, she waited
until the housekeeper had finished her purchase and
placed the parcel of fish in her basket, then she moved
forward and touched her arm.

'Excuse me, Signora, may I speak to you, please?'

The woman turned and Petra was so surprised to see
the look of fear that came into the woman's face that
she stood stock still and Maria began to hurry away.
Realising that she might lose her, Petra ran after the
woman and grabbed her arm, holding it firmly when
the woman tried to pull away.

'No, no.' Maria said agitatedly, but was encumbered
by her heavy basket. 'You go. I not speak.'

'But I only want to ask you a few questions.' Petra
kept a tight hold of her arm and firmly led her outside.
The woman's reaction surprised Petra and also
frightened her. Why was Maria so afraid? Perhaps if she
found the answer to that she would also find the answer
to where Sara had gone. 'You remember I came to the
palazzo yesterday?' she said with a smile, trying to put
the other woman at her ease.

Maria nodded reluctantly. '*Si.* I remember you.'

'I wanted to ask Count Berini about a friend of mine,
Sara Hamling. Look, here's her photograph.' Groping
in her bag with her free hand, Petra pulled out a
snapshot of Sara and herself taken only a few months
ago. 'Sara is the blonde girl,' she said unnecessarily,
holding the photo under Maria's nose. 'Have you seen
her before?'

The woman glanced at the photograph and her face
went white. But she shook her head. 'No. I no see her.'

'But you must have done,' Petra protested. 'She came
to stay at the Palazzo. About two weeks ago.'

'No. I no see.' Maria pulled frantically to free her arm, her basket tipping dangerously. 'I go now.' A green pepper rolled from her basket as she at last jerked her arm from Petra's hold, and then she was hurrying away, almost running in her haste, more vegetables falling as she went.

'Hey wait!' Petra stooped to pick them up, but by the time she straightened up Maria had disappeared back into the crowds in the big market. So what was she supposed to make of that? It was obvious that the woman was lying. And she had looked so scared. That aspect of it troubled Petra more than anything else. Was she afraid of what Count Berini would do if she admitted having seen Sara? Or was Maria afraid because she knew what had happened to her?

Petra's blood ran cold. She ran after Maria but it was too late, there was no sign of her in the busy alleyways. That was the trouble with Venice, there were so many small squares with a dozen alleys opening out of them. Maria, presumably being a native, would know a hundred different ways back to the palazzo. Petra ran back that way in the hope of catching her before she got inside, but there were tourists as well as shoppers about now and it was impossible to really hurry, and once, in her haste, Petra took a wrong turning and had to retrace her steps. Breathless, she arrived at the high wall surrounding the palazzo but there was no sign of Maria. She hung around for about an hour just in case she'd got there first, but then admitted defeat and went back to the café. It was time, she decided, to get a little help.

Vasco got three hours off in the afternoons, from three until six, in between serving lunches and early dinners. At three, Petra had got hold of him and told him all about Sara, by four she had persuaded him to help her and at four-thirty they were strolling as casually as they could down to the alley alongside the palazzo, Vasco carrying a wooden ladder that had once been very long but had broken and now only had half-a-dozen rungs. When they reached the alley, Petra kept watch at the entrance while Vasco placed the ladder against the wall where they could see the trees growing over the top. Then Petra ran back to him and prepared to climb up. 'Don't forget; come back in half an hour,' she reminded him anxiously.

'*Si*. But I should go in the garden, not you.'

'No; we agreed; you don't know what to look for.' It had gone against Vasco's burgeoning manly pride when Petra had insisted that she climb into the garden herself.

Quickly she climbed up, praying that no one would come out of the palazzo into the alley while she was doing so. Her head drew level with the top of the wall and Petra looked cautiously over, but there was very little to see, just the trees and a glimpse of a water garden with stone statues. She hoisted herself on top of the wall, gave Vasco a wave, then lowered herself to hang by her hands and drop on to the soft earth on the other side.

Her heart thumping, Petra picked herself up and looked around. The garden was small for such a large house, barely a quarter of an acre, but it was pleasant and well-cared for, obviously designed to provide shade from the hot Adriatic sun. Trying to move as quietly and unobtrusively as possible, she crept towards the house, careful to keep in the shade and as much under cover as she could in case anyone was looking out of a window. She wished she knew whether Carlo Berini was definitely at home or not; they had peered round the end of the alley and the motorboat wasn't there so the chances were that he was out, but Petra would have been a hundred times happier if she had known for certain.

She had no definite idea of what she was going to do, perhaps try to get hold of Maria again and try to talk to her, but at least have a good look round for any trace of Sara. The ground floor windows at the back of the palazzo were low windows with little stone balconies and one room had double doors that opened on to the garden. Petra inched her way to the shrub nearest to the house and crouched in its shelter, gathering up her courage before she ran across the open space to the first window. Gingerly she lifted her head and peeped in, to be immediately disappointed; this was just a large kitchen and Maria wasn't there.

Slowly she worked her way to the left, trying to make as little noise as possible. The next two windows looked into a big dining-room, all the furniture and decor as magnificent as the part of the house Petra had already seen. The french doors came next with a wide step below them. It took quite a bit of nerve to creep up to them and peek round the edge, and she had to lift a hand to shield her eyes from the sun reflected in the glass, so that she could see better. The room was empty and she gave a sigh of relief; Carlo Berini wasn't there—but then neither was Sara. The room looked like a library, its walls covered mostly by shelves full of richly bound and very heavy-looking books. At the rest of the windows Petra again drew a blank and she stood up, feeling completely frustrated. Now what? It looked as if climbing into the garden had been a complete waste of time.

Feeling more confident now that she knew the ground floor rooms were empty, Petra went back to the french windows and tried them experimentally, but as she'd expected they were locked. The only other thing left was a door near the kitchen which must give access to the servants' quarters. Petra tried it but that, too, was locked. She stood there, glaring at the door, her hands on her hips, wishing that she could kick it down in her frustration. Raising her head, Petra looked up at the first floor windows, wondering whether it would be possible for her to climb up and look in them.

'I really wouldn't try it, if I were you,' a grim, masculine voice said behind her.

Petra whirled round, completely startled, not having heard a sound. The sun was in her eyes and for an instant all she could make out was the dark bulk of someone looming over her like a bird of prey, its outline hazed by the sunlight. But then she blinked and knew who it was. A swift look at the open french window told her how Carlo Berini had got into the garden, but she could hardly believe that she hadn't heard anything. He must move like a cat. She backed nervously away from him, her throat too dry to speak.

'How did you get in here?' he demanded.

'I—I climbed over the wall.'

'By yourself? You couldn't have done.' His eyes went over her slight figure in tight jeans and T-shirt.

Not wanting him to find out about Vasco, she said, 'Yes, I did. I'm—I'm very good at that kind of thing.'

His mouth thinned and it was obvious that he didn't believe her, but he let it go. 'I suppose I need hardly ask why you're here.'

'I'm looking for Sara. Why don't you tell me where she is?' Petra challenged, remembering that attack is the best form of defence. 'Just what have you got to hide, Count Berini?'

He didn't show any reaction other than slightly sardonic amusement. 'Why won't you accept my word,

Miss Thornton?' he countered. 'And just what are you
going to do now?'

Petra stared at him, realising what an ambiguous
situation she was in. She couldn't climb back over the
wall without help and a great loss of dignity, and Carlo
Berini was barring the way to the french doors. He took
a menacing step towards her. 'Do you realise that I
could have you arrested for breaking in here?'

Somehow she managed to stand her ground. 'I
haven't broken in,' she objected stubbornly. 'And if you
call the police I'll tell them about Sara.'

'So you haven't been to them yet?'

'No, but I intend to. And the British Consul,' she
added, trying to impress him.

But it didn't; his mouth merely curled sarcastically.
'You terrify me,' he mocked.

'Well, you should be,' Petra exclaimed, angry now.
'Because I mean it. I know that Sara's been here and
that you're lying to me. And I intend to go on until I
find Sara. 'I *won't* give up until I do,' she threatened.

'You must be very fond of your friend.'

'I am. She's—very special.'

The look on Carlo Berini's face changed, became
appraising as his eyes again ran over her boyish figure,
and Petra flushed deeply as she realised what he was
thinking. 'We've known each other all our lives. We're
more like sisters,' she retorted defensively, although why
she found it necessary to have to tell him she didn't know.

An angry frown came into his eyes. 'I have already
told you several times that I know nothing whatsoever
about your friend.'

'And I've told *you* that I don't believe you.'

The frown deepened into an arrogant sneer. 'I am not
in the habit of having my word questioned—by
anyone!'

'Really?' Petra put a wealth of insult into the one word.

Real anger flashed into his dark eyes and he took a hasty step towards her. Petra backed up precipitately, but was brought up short by the wall of the house. 'I'm growing extremely tired of your insults, Signorina. You will leave here at once and if I find you here again I will have no hesitation in handing you over to the police.'

Petra stared up at him, her back pressed against the wall, afraid of his anger but mesmerised by his eyes that seemed to pierce into her. 'What have you done to Sara?' Her voice rose rather hysterically as she repeated it. 'What have you done to Sara?'

'I've never even set eyes on her. Will nothing I say convince you?'

'No. But ...' Petra looked at him calculatingly, wondering if she dare. 'But I might be convinced, if you would let me search the palazzo for myself.'

Carlo Berini's eyes widened in surprise. 'You can't be serious?'

'Yes, I am. Do you think I'd make such a suggestion for fun?'

'To make the suggestion at all is an insult. Do you really think that I permit anyone who walks in and demands to search the palazzo to do so?'

'I don't know. How many people do you get who want to? If what you say is true you can have no objection whatsoever to me searching the place,' she pointed out reasonably.

His jaw tightened. 'You are becoming a nuisance, Signorina Thornton. I suggest you leave Venice and stay away.'

Petra was about to make an indignant retort but stopped as she saw a woman step out of the french doors into the garden. She was older than Petra, about twenty-eight, perhaps even a well-preserved thirty, and her figure was fuller, but she was very elegantly dressed, her dark hair sleeked back from a face whose features were much enhanced by the skilful use of make-up. But it all added up to a very sophisticated image. The woman spoke to Carlo Berini in Italian, looking curiously at Petra.

The Count frowned when he saw her and replied quickly, while Petra stood silently by, knowing that they were talking about her and feeling very plain and about sixteen years old with her unmade-up face and old jeans. She caught the word 'Inglese' and she thought he called the woman Francesca, but that was all she understood. A growing resentment at being talked about as if she wasn't there, especially in a foreign language, filled her, but there was little she could do about it except glare at them antagonistically. Unfortunately she was the intruder and she couldn't just walk away as she would like to have done.

Carlo Berini turned back to her and gave a thin smile when he saw her outraged face. 'Little girls who go where they shouldn't must expect what they get,' he informed her with soft derision. Then, curtly, 'Follow me.' Turning on his heel, he led the way through the french doors and Petra obeyed, her chin high as she passed the other woman who watched her in surprised interest, as if she couldn't possibly believe that she had actually come into contact with such a creature. When they entered the palazzo, Petra hung back, her eyes darting around for any sign of Sara having been there, although what she hoped to find she had no idea.

At the door, Carlo Berini looked round and his eyebrows rose sardonically as he realised what she was doing. Coming over, he took hold of her firmly by the arm and walked her briskly through the big hall to the side door.

'All right, I'm going. You don't have to manhandle me!' she exclaimed indignantly, rubbing her arm when he let her go, although he hadn't hurt her.

He laughed rather cruelly. 'Don't exaggerate. If I decided to manhandle you, as you call it, you'd really know that you'd been touched.' His eyes met hers and held for a long menacing moment before he said, 'Out, Signorina Thornton, and I don't want to see you again. And it will do you no good to climb over into the garden a second time. The house is wired with burglar alarms and you set one off when you touched the windows,' he told her grimly as he opened the big wooden door. Petra looked up at him mutinuously, knowing that she'd failed and unwilling to plead. His face softened a little. 'You must look for your friend somewhere else. Please accept that she is not here and has never been here.'

'I won't ever do that. Not until I find her,' Petra declared passionately, then turned and ran into the alley.

Vasco was hanging around the end of the narrow lane, watching out for her anxiously. His face was a picture when he saw that she'd come out of the door. 'What happened? Were you—did the Count find you? I put the rope over the wall but you did not pull the ladder over.'

'No. Come on, I'll tell you about it, but let's get away from here first.'

They hurried back to the courtyard behind the café and put the ladder back where they'd found it, untying the rope that they'd intended to use to pull the ladder over the wall so that Petra could climb back into the alley. Then they went up to the top floor, sat on the top step of the stairs, and Petra recounted what had happened to her.

'He did not sent for the *polizia*?' Vasco asked in amazement.

'No, he just warned me off.'

'Maybe he speak true. Maybe your friend does not go to the Palazzo Berini.'

Petra sighed. 'I don't have any proof either way. All I have is what Sara told me. And she had no reason to lie or to make it up, now had she?'

Vasco didn't quite understand so Petra put it more simply and he nodded. 'But what you do now?'

'I don't know. Just keep on watching the place, I suppose. Vasco, that woman who was there, I think her name is Francesca; do you know her?'

'No, but I have heard something. She is not of Venice but of Padua, I think.'

'Is Count Berini engaged to her—will he marry her?' she substituted when he frowned.

He shrugged eloquently. 'Who knows? He is a deep one, the Count. But he must marry soon. For a son, you understand. Perhaps it may be this one you speak of, perhaps not. He is not an easy man to satisfy.'

'But he likes women?'

The question caused Vasco to laugh delightedly. 'But of course. He is Italian, is he not? But even more than that he is a Venetian!'

Which in Vasco's eyes anyway, was really saying something; the Latin lover to end all Latin lovers, obviously.

Petra grinned. 'Try and think of what I can do next; I can't just hang around the palazzo indefinitely, hoping to find a clue.'

Vasco wasn't much help, but then Petra couldn't think of anything either. Her mind went round and round the problem; had she made a mistake? had she misheard what Sara had said before she drove away with her rich pick-up? That thought made something click in her brain and she turned excitedly to the young Venetian. 'Vasco, surely some of the people in Venice own cars?'

'Yes, of course. Many do.'

'But where do they keep them? There aren't any in Venice itself.'

'No. You drive across the bridge from Venice Mestre and leave all cars at the Piazzale Roma, near the station. You catch there also the autobus for Mestre.'

'And Count Berini, does he have a car there?'

'*Si*. He has a car.'

'You don't—oh, Vasco, you don't know what kind of car he has, do you?' Petra asked breathlessly.

But he shook his head. 'No. He take his boat to Piazzale. Then take his car. I never see it.'

Petra sighed, remembering the boat's powerful lines. Impossible to follow that. But perhaps she could go to the Piazzale Roma and wait in the hope of the Count coming there to collect his car. But that would be very chancy; it had to be a big and busy area and she might easily miss him. Resting her chin on her hands, Petra tried to work it out, then she sat up straight, 'Vasco, can you get hold of a boat?'

CHAPTER THREE

VASCO was extremely reluctant to help her again and it took quite a bit of persuasion plus her repeated assurances that she hadn't told the Count anything about him, before he at length agreed that he could borrow a boat from a friend for a while.

'Tonight?'

He nodded. '*Si*. Tonight.'

Vasco went off to telephone while Petra went into the café for a meal. They didn't have a very varied menu; just four different kinds of pizza, pasta, and sandwiches. She ordered spaghetti bolognese and Emilio brought her up a huge plateful, together with a bread roll and a sideplate of chips. It was far more than she'd expected, but Emilio used his hands in expressive sign language by pointing at her and then bringing his hands down first in dead straight lines and then in exaggerated double curves to explain that she was far too thin and that he was going to fatten her up. Petra looked at the steaming pile of food and decided that she would have to eat elsewhere if she didn't want to be killed by kindness. Emilio's ideal female figure wasn't everyone's and she did have *some* curves, for heaven's sake. She was hungry and ate quite a lot, but had to leave some of the spaghetti and most of the roll and chips. Emilio shook his head over her, but she grinned at him and patted her stomach to show how full it was.

There was an hour yet before it would be dark, so Petra strolled down to St Mark's Square, still thronged with sightseers, even though most of the day trippers had gone home, the tourists back to their hotels and the visitors from the cruise liners back to their ships. There were still people queuing to go up to the top of the Campanile, to enter the Clock Tower and to have their photograph taken feeding the pigeons. Ordinarily Petra would have been entranced by Venice, but she couldn't look at it with the eyes of a tourist, finding herself wondering whether Sara had walked in the Square, if she had fed the pigeons or sat at one of the café tables and listened to the music from the small orchestra that played light classical tunes for the benefit of both their customers and passers-by. Petra sat on a low wall near the canal and waited impatiently for the sun to start to set, unable to appreciate the beauty and history of the scene before her, across the canal to the huge church of San Giorgio with its own campanile tower, or back down the Grand Canal to the Academy bridge. When the sun sank low behind the red roofs of Venice, turning the waters of the canal into a river of blood, Petra stood up and hurried to meet Vasco. He had managed to leave the café early and was waiting for her, leading her down alleyways and across canals until she was completely lost, but after only ten minutes or so they emerged on to a path, a *fondamenta*, Vasco called it, running alongside a small and very smelly canal. Beside it was a kind of boatyard where several gondolas and other, less glamorous craft were in various stages of repair. A boy about the same age as Vasco came out of a nearby house and the two talked together while Petra waited in the background, then Vasco called her over and the other youth led them to the boat they were to borrow.

Petra looked at it with some misgivings. It was an old gondola, its sides scored by numerous encounters with canal walls in which it had definitely come off worst, and there was also a puddle of water in the bottom. 'Will it stay afloat?' she demanded dubiously.

'But yes. Is good boat.'

They found a cushion for her and Petra got in while Vasco stood behind her and fitted the pole into the specially carved rowlock. The gondola wobbled a bit from side to side of the narrow waterway as they set off, several times coming dangerously close to scraping the side.

'Have you ever done this before?' she asked rather breathlessly.

Vasco laughed. 'Maybe three-four times. But I am not—expert.' They came up to a bridge and he had to hastily get down on his knees to get under it because he'd gone too close to the side.

Turning her head in dismay, Petra found him grinning at her, a grin she was unable to resist, so that she laughed back at him and hung on as they weaved their unsteady way out into a larger canal.

Pushing his pole hard against the bottom, Vasco shot them forward and they emerged suddenly into the Grand Canal—almost under the bows of a vaporetto, which hooted stridently. Vasco hastily dug his pole into the water to stop them and nearly overbalanced. Petra clung to the side and prayed fervently that they wouldn't be overturned. The old gondola rocked wildly in the wash of the larger boat and the puddle in the bottom grew bigger, but it must have been stouter than it looked because it didn't turn over or sink. Vasco poled on, more cautiously now, and Petra looked for some familiar landmark, but it was completely alien in the dark. Then, 'There it is, the Palazzo Berini,' Vasco told her.

Looking forward, Petra saw the gothic doorway of the palace, lit on either side by ornate electric lamps, the

motor boat still tied up in front of it. Vasco turned out
their own light and they glided up to the boat on the far
side from the house. Vasco caught hold of the other
boat and Petra climbed quickly over, opened the cabin
door and slipped inside. Then Vasco immediately
pushed off and she saw him put his light on again after
he'd moved on about twenty yards or so. She tried to
watch his light as he turned the boat but it merged with
the bright lights of a restaurant on the other side and
she lost it. So then there was nothing to do except make
herself as comfortable as possible and hope that Count
Berini would be using his car tonight, otherwise she had
a long wait.

The cabin was quite large, big enough to take four
people in comfort, the seats upholstered in soft leather
that smelt new. There were windows all round the cabin
with curtains tied back with cords, and when a
motoscafo passed with all its lights on, Petra caught the
reflection of shining chrome fittings, but she didn't dare
turn on the light to examine her surroundings more
closely and had to stay in the dark. As time passed the
traffic on the canal dwindled away, the couples taking
romantic moonlit gondola rides had gone back to their
hotels for, hopefully, the natural outcome, and the
restaurants were turning out their lights. Petra saw the
'Venice by Night' boat returning to the Piazzetta near
the Doge's Palace and knew that it must be nearly
eleven thirty. She sighed and stretched, wishing the
cabin was high enough to stand up in. Her vigil tonight
had been a waste of time, but Vasco had promised to
come and pick her up at midnight.

A brighter light filled the cabin. Glancing swiftly
towards the palazzo, Petra saw that the big door had
opened and Count Berini stood on the threshold. A
minute later he was joined by the woman, Francesca,

who'd been with him earlier that day. Petra bobbed
down out of sight and prayed that Francesca wouldn't
come into the cabin.

Luckily she didn't. Carlo Berini helped her aboard,
untied the ropes and then the beautiful boat came alive,
like a leopard that had wakened from sleep, its power
evident in each throb of the engine. It curved out into
the canal and surged forward, its nose lifting out of the
water as the Count accelerated, the broad beam of the
boat's powerful headlight splitting the darkness ahead.
Risking a look through the window, Petra saw the two
of them standing together in the cockpit. The woman
was in evening dress now and there was a small
weekend case on the floor behind her. As Petra watched,
Count Berini put a casual arm round her waist and
drew her closer to him. She went willingly enough and
smiled up at him with what Petra decided was an
extremely cloying look. Yeuk! Petra looked away,
feeling suddenly angry. Did the silly female have to
throw herself at him like that? Okay, maybe he was
good looking and sexually attractive and magnetic
and . . . Her thoughts came to a sudden halt. Just when
had she decided all those things about him? So far all
she'd seen of Carlo Berini was arrogance and anger. But
even that, together with all the lies he'd told her, hadn't
blinded her to the fact that he was very attractive to
women. He had everything it took, including money;
Petra would be willing to bet that he could even be
charming when it suited him, only that was a side of
him that she was unlikely ever to see. Not that she
wanted to; all she wanted was to find Sara and go
home.

The engine slowed and the boat nosed its way
skilfully into some kind of boathouse, its dark interior
gradually revealed as the headlight pierced the shadows.

Petra hastily got down on the floor but risked a peek through the starboard window when the boat rocked as Count Berini got off to make it fast. What she saw made her catch her breath and held her transfixed. The boathouse also doubled as a garage and there, only a few feet away, was a powerful sports car. A red one. The same car that she'd seen from the apartment window on the night that Sara had left!

The boat rocked again as he helped Francesca out and then the Count came back on board to get her case. Petra jerked back to life and bobbed down again, staying there until she heard the door on the land side of the building being opened, the car driven out and then the door closed again, leaving her in darkness. She gave them what she judged were ten minutes, just in case they came back for anything, then decided it was safe to leave. She felt excited and triumphant, completely sure now that Count Berini had been lying, and ready to take her story to the authorities. She would go first thing in the morning. But now she had better get back to the café. If, as she guessed, this private boathouse was near the Piazzale Roma, then she had a long walk ahead of her. Petra turned the handle of the cabin door—and found that it was locked!

For a few minutes she couldn't believe it. She jerked the handle up and down in case it had just got stuck and then tried pushing the door, but neither did any good. So now what was she supposed to do? Groping for the seat, Petra found it and sat down. It was completely dark and she didn't like it. Before she had had all the lights along the canal for company, but now she found it difficult to even try to work things out rationally in the darkness. But she must think, concentrate. Vasco had said that he thought Francesca came from Padua. If that was so and she'd been staying with Carlo Berini, then it could be that he was driving her home. But that didn't help very much because she had no very clear idea where Padua was. It could be a couple of hundred miles away for all she knew. Petra saw herself being imprisoned here for hours on end and wished that she'd paid more attention to the map of Italy in geography lessons at school. A thought occurred to her that made her blood run cold; what if the two of them had gone on holiday or something together? She could be here for weeks! She'd starve to death!

Petra gave a low moan and had another, rather frantic go at the door, then remembered the windows and tried them, but they seemed to be sealed; she couldn't find any way to open them in the darkness. She felt like screaming for help but realised that there probably wouldn't be anyone around to hear at this time of night. She would just have to wait till the morning; maybe then she could find a way out. Curling up as comfortably as she could on the cabin seat, Petra prepared to wait it out.

The sound of the engine starting up precipitated her into wakefulness. She started up in a fright and then gave a hastily swallowed cry of pain as she forgot where she was and banged her head on the roof. The big spotlight in the bow came on and she saw that the car was back. The boat was reversed out into the Grand Canal and was driven even faster this time. Carlo Berini was standing at the wheel, legs apart to brace himself as they surged along, their speed creating white waves of wash on either side. Presumably the Count had taken his girlfriend to Padua and was now going home. Which meant that she'd be stuck outside the palazzo until Vasco somehow managed to rescue her.

The motor boat was turned in a smooth, graceful

curve and stopped within an inch of the steps outside the Palazzo Berini, where the lights were still on. Petra ducked down out of sight and managed to look at her watch; two o'clock in the morning. She heard the Count moving about and presumed he was making the boat fast and turning off the lights. Then he would go in and she would be left to wait again. But instead of going inside, he unlocked the cabin door, the lifebelts from the sides of the boat in his hands, ready to stow them in the cabin. Petra stopped breathing in the hope that he wouldn't see or hear her, but the next second the cabin light was switched on. Carlo Berini was staring at her in astonishment. 'Good God! How long have you been there?' Then his face hardened. 'I'm beginning to get extremely tired of your spying, Signorina.' He dropped the lifebelts on to a seat and stood back. 'Come on out.'

'Er—if it's all the same to you ...' Petra began nervously.

'Out,' he repeated in a voice that wasn't to be disobeyed.

She edged past him and stepped quickly on to the stone steps outside the palazzo, wishing fervently that there was somewhere to run to, but short of jumping into the canal and swimming for it there was no way of escaping him. Berini didn't hurry; he locked the cabin and checked that the boat was securely moored before joining her on the steps and reaching up to take a big, ornate key from a high stone shelf above the doorway. After unlocking the great wooden doors, he pushed them open and said, with heavy sarcasm, 'Welcome to the Palazzo Berini once more, Signorina Thornton.'

Petra couldn't move. She stood there tensely, her hands balled into tight, frightened fists at her sides, staring at him.

His voice grew mocking. 'Afraid, signorina?'

After a moment she found her voice and managed to
say, 'I have every reason to be afraid of you.'

The Count's expression changed. 'Yes, I suppose
from your point of view you have, but I assure you that
you have nothing to fear.' He paused but when she
didn't speak, went on, 'My housekeeper is in the
palazzo; you have only to ring the bell or call and she
will come. And really,' he added rather harshly when
she didn't move, 'what choice do you have? You must
either walk through the house to get to the street door
or stay out here on the steps all night.'

He was right, there was no other way. Petra moved
slowly towards the doorway but hesitated as she came
up to where he stood, raising her head to look into his
face. If his expression had been the least threatening she
would probably have started screaming there and then,
but to her surprise there was only amusement in his
eyes, sardonic amusement, maybe, in the curl of his thin
lips, but nothing to increase her fears. Petra stepped
past him into the entrance to the palazzo feeling rather
like a fly who was voluntarily entering the spider's
parlour.

There was already a single lamp left burning but he
pressed some switches and the place was suddenly
flooded with light. Despite her apprehension Petra gave
a gasp of amazement at the richness of the entrance
hall. There was marble everywhere, from the tessellated
floor up to the arches that supported the ceiling and
rose in a graceful, pillared sweep up the grand staircase,
but the coldness of the stone was warmed by the rich
colours of tapestries and paintings on the walls and by
the frescoes that ran riot on the ceiling and up each
section of the staircase.

The Count let her gaze for a couple of minutes, then
said, 'Shall we go up?'

His voice made her jump. Petra turned quickly round to look at him again but his expression hadn't changed. She opened her mouth to refuse, to demand to be taken to the street door and head for the safety of the café, but then she remembered Sara. Only this man knew where she was and could tell her where to find her, and running away wasn't going to help, so when he gestured towards the staircase she went slowly up ahead of him. He showed her into the same room where she'd been before, but this time he didn't go to sit behind his desk, instead crossing to a sidetable where decanters were set out on a large ornate silver tray. 'Would you like a drink?'

'No. No, thank you,' she amended, incurably polite.

He gave a small smile and poured one for himself, the ice clinking in the crystal tumbler. Then he turned. 'And I suppose you don't want to sit down either? No, I thought not, but you must excuse me if I do.' He sat in a deep leather armchair, his legs stretched out in front of him and looked at her over his glass as he took a drink. Petra stood nervously near the door, still poised to run if he made a move towards her. But he merely said rather resignedly, 'All right, Signorina Thornton, now tell me why you were in my boat.'

'You—you know why.'

'To look for your friend presumably. But did you seriously believe that she might be on my boat?'

'No. No, of course not.' Petra hesitated, wondering how much to tell him. She didn't want to give everything away, but on the other hand he might be forced into telling the truth. 'I hid on your boat because I hoped you might be taking your—er—fiancée home, and I wanted to see what kind of car you drive.'

'And why should that interest you?'

'Because Sara was given a lift to Venice. And she told me what kind of car it was. I even saw it myself.'

The Count had grown still, his eyes fixed intently on her face. 'And what kind of car was it?'

'A Ferrari. A blood-red Ferrari.' Petra shivered as she remembered Sara's excited voice saying those words.

'And I, of course, own exactly the same car.'

'Yes.' She gazed at him, wondering if this was the same man she'd seen out of the window that night. It could be, the Count was both tall and dark, but the man's face had been shadowed and she hadn't seen it properly. If only she'd insisted that Sara hadn't gone with him, or she'd gone down to see him for herself.

He was looking at Petra reflectively. 'So you have yet another reason to be afraid of me. And yet you let me bring you in here. Surely a very foolish—or else a very brave thing to do?'

'I want to find Sara. Where is she?' Petra demanded bluntly.

He put down his drink and leaned forward, smiling grimly when she instinctively took a step backwards. 'I'm sorry, Signorina, but I just don't know. But obviously it distresses me that you should have these suspicions of me, and it makes me angry to think that someone has used my name to—shall we say, lure your friend to go with him.'

'And did he use your car, too?' Petra asked jeeringly, her courage beginning to return a little.

'That, as you say, would seem to be a damning coincidence,' he agreed. 'But Ferraris are made in Italy and many men in Venice drive them. It is one of the most popular sports cars, you understand?'

She didn't say anything but it was perfectly obvious that she didn't believe him.

'I am not in the habit of having my word doubted,' he informed her coldly.

'No?'

Her tone was insulting and he frowned, showing anger for the first time. 'You had better start at the beginning and tell me exactly why you thought your friend was here. And please sit down; your continuing to stand is . . .' he shrugged, 'understandable but ridiculous. I'm not a wolf, Signorina Thornton, I'm not going to eat you.'

Reluctantly, Petra moved to a chair opposite him and perched on the edge, like a bird ready to fly away at the first hint of danger.

Count Berini again gave that small, not really amused smile, and said, 'Now, tell me.'

'You already know everything; a tall, dark man met Sara in Paris and offered to drive her to Venice. He gave your name and your address and he drove . . .'

'. . . a blood-red Ferrari. Yes, that I know,' the Count agreed wryly. 'But did you see this man yourself, or the number of his car?'

Petra shook her head unhappily. 'No, only from a distance.'

'When was this exactly?'

'Earlier this month. Sara left early in the morning of the fourth and she phoned me on the . . .'

She broke off as the Count gave an exclamation of satisfaction. 'The fourth you said? Then I can prove that this man was an impostor. I was in America then.'

'Am-America?' Petra stared at him, feeling slightly stunned.

'Yes. I can even show you my passport with the date stamps on it, if you wish.'

'Yes, please,' Petra accepted without hesitation.

For a moment his nostrils flared and he looked as

aristocratic as his ancestry entitled him to be. She thought he was going to make some remark about doubting his word again, but instead he gave a slight shrug and crossed over to his desk, taking a small bunch of keys from his pocket and unlocking the top drawer. He looked inside for a moment and then stopped and gave a short laugh. 'I'm afraid I can't after all. I've just remembered that my passport had almost run out when I returned from America so I immediately sent it to be renewed. I will, of course, be happy to show it to you when it is returned to me.'

'But then the date stamps won't be on it, will they, if it's a new passport?' Petra pointed out, up on her feet again and her old suspicions increased a hundredfold.

Count Berini looked at her across the desk, his expression unreadable. 'Possibly not,' he agreed.

A clock in the room began to chime three, making her jump. 'Good heavens! Is that the time? I really must be going,' she exclaimed and headed for the door like a guest who'd had enough of a dull party, but the Count's voice brought her to a halt as she reached to open it.

'Signorina Thornton, I shall say this just once more and that will be the final time; I have never set eyes on your friend. I did not meet her in Paris nor drive her back to this house. I was not even in this country on the date you mentioned. To all this I give you my word, the word of a Berini. Which may mean little to you,' he added grimly, 'but counts for much, not only in Venice, but the whole of Italy, and wherever in the world I do business.'

Her hand still on the doorknob, Petra turned to face him.' Her eyes searched his face as he looked steadily back at her. She realised, suddenly, just how devastatingly attractive he was and wondered if Sara, too, had . . . Her chin came up. 'I'm sorry,' she said clearly and firmly. 'I would like to accept your word, but obviously I can't without proof. Not when Sara's— safety might depend on it.'

The Count's features became cold and withdrawn. 'I do not enjoy being called a liar.'

'I'm sorry,' Petra said defensively, but somehow knowing that *she* shouldn't be on the defensive.

To her surprise he gave a very Italian shrug of his shoulders. 'It is hardly your fault, but the fault of the man who used my name. And that is why, Signorina, I must insist on helping you to find your friend.'

Petra's eyes widened in surprise. '*Help* me to find Sara?'

'That is what you want, isn't it?'

'Well yes, but *you* . . .'

'I am not a monster, Signorina,' he pointed out exasperatedly. 'And I get as angry as the next man when I am falsely accused of being a liar and a—what? What do you think I did to your friend? Abducted her? Kidnapped her? Or even murdered her? At the very least you must think that I seduced her.'

As Petra had thought all those things, her vivid imagination painting the most horrifying pictures, she could only stand dumbly until he nodded. 'I see that I'm right. Well, perhaps luckily for both of us, I am not without some power in Venice. If your friend ever really came here I should be able to find out.'

'What do you mean, really came here?' Petra asked, curious despite her misgivings.

'This man who used my name; he could have driven your friend anywhere. I'm sorry, but there it is.'

'But Sara would have told me that when she phoned me, surely?'

His eyes met hers intently. 'Are you saying that she phoned you *after* she left for Venice?'

'Yes. A few days later.'

'And what did she say exactly?'

Petra hesitated, again in a fix about how much to tell him. 'Nothing,' she said finally, lamely.

The Count's mouth set into a grim line. 'Will you never trust me?'

'I—I don't have any reason to.'

Shaking his head as though he couldn't really believe it, he said, almost to himself, 'Never in my life have I been in such a position.' And then, directly at her, 'I think it is time, Signorina, that I took you home. Nothing is going to be gained by continuing this argument until I can prove to you that I don't know your friend.' Coming round from behind the desk he opened the door for her. 'And not until then will we make any progress in finding her.'

Awkwardly Petra said, 'Look, even if you could prove that you didn't know Sara, I wouldn't want you to . . .'

'. . . to help you find her. Then you would be a fool, for I don't think you will have any success by yourself.'

He spoke over his shoulder as he led the way down the marble staircase, through the smaller hall and to the street door. He held it open for her, waiting to follow her through, but Petra stopped just outside, glad to be out of the palazzo at last. 'I can manage on my own now, thanks,' she assured him. 'You really don't have to come with me.'

Count Berini gave a derisive laugh. 'Anyone less able to take care of herself I have never met. If you could you would never have hidden on my boat, or at least not alone. Didn't it ever cross your mind that I might find you? And have every right to be angry when I did? Especially given the suspicions you had of me.'

That it hadn't occurred to her made Petra say huffily, 'I've said I'll go alone.'

'You might have said it but there's no way I will allow it. Where are you staying?' he demanded, taking a firm grip on her arm and thwarting the budding idea she'd had to turn and run.

'It's only a few minutes away. I'll be quite all right, honestly.'

'Then we'll soon be there.' And he began to walk quickly up the alleyway, pulling her along with him.

There was no choice but to tell him about the café and they had soon walked through the deserted lanes, their footsteps echoing eerily in the ancient sleeping city. When they reached the back of the café he waited to make sure the door had been left unlocked for her.

'Thank you for walking me home,' Petra said with a formality that she knew sounded ridiculous. 'Goodbye.'

'Oh not goodbye, Signorina,' Count Berini said mockingly. 'Merely *arrivederci*. For I am quite sure that we are going to see more of each other, you and I.'

CHAPTER FOUR

IT was only the liberal use of Peter Dudley's name that enabled Petra to see anyone of importance at the British Consulate the next morning. The place was short staffed due apparently to it being the last day of a trade fair, and it was quite crowded with people who waited impatiently for help. Petra had to explain several times that she hadn't lost her passport or run out of money and was eventually shown into the office of someone higher than just a clerk.

The man behind the desk was younger than she expected; in his late twenties Petra guessed, and he stood up and gave her a friendly smile, reaching out to shake her hand. 'Hallo, I'm Tony Reid. I gather you've got a problem that's a bit out of the ordinary?'

'That's right.' Petra sat down in a comfortable chair by his desk, relieved that she'd reached someone who seemed capable of giving her some attention. 'My friend seems to have disappeared.' His eyebrows rose disbelievingly and Petra quickly explained. 'So you see,' she finished, 'the only clue I have is this Count Berini and he denies all knowledge of having seen Sara.'

Tony Reid had been taking notes while she'd been talking, his smile changing to a frown. 'Tell me exactly what the Count said to you.' Petra did so and his frown deepened. 'I hate to have to say this, but your Count Berini is one of the most powerful men in Venice. His family goes back to the founding of the city, and at least two of his ancestors were elected as Doge. More, probably, if you think of the way the great families intermarried. If it was almost anyone else we could bring some pressure to bear, but not with him, I'm afraid. All we can do is ask politely and hope that he's willing to co-operate.'

'He did say that he was going to help me to find Sara—whether I liked it or not,' Petra revealed.

'Did he?' The young diplomat's eyebrows rose. 'Sounds pretty autocratic. Is that the way he struck you?'

Thinking back to her forced interview with the Count last night, Petra nodded. 'He was very—arrogant. He gave the impression that being mixed up in anything so—so sordid, was an insult.'

'Hmm. But he'd give that impression even if he was guilty, wouldn't he?'

Petra smiled at him warmly, gratified that he was thinking along the same lines as she was. 'That's exactly what I thought.'

Tony Reid grinned back at her and Petra felt an instinctive liking for him, a feeling that she could trust him, that he wouldn't let her down. He was nice looking in a very English way, with brown hair and eyes and a fair complexion, nothing dramatic but very nice, the sort of person your mother would be happy to see you marry. He glanced at his watch. 'If you like, I'll go and see Berini myself. If he knows you've got the weight of the Consulate behind you he might be a bit more forthcoming. And we've got some contacts at the airport who might remember him either leaving for America or coming back. He didn't give you the exact dates he said he was away, did he?' And when Petra shook her head, 'Well, never mind. He's a well-known figure round Venice; someone might well remember him. Excuse me for a few minutes.' Lifting up the phone, he made several quick calls, speaking in rapid, and to Petra, quite unintelligible, Italian, then stood up. 'Let's go then, shall we?'

As they walked through the tourist-crowded streets Tony, as he told her to call him, asked her about her home and family and Petra answered him quite happily and naturally and they were soon chatting as if they'd known each other for years. They were of the same class and kind and Petra felt completely at home with him. He pointed out several places of interest as they went along and asked Petra what she thought of Venice.

'I'm afraid I haven't really seen any of it yet,' she confessed. 'All I've done since I arrived here is look for Sara. Somehow it doesn't seem right to just behave like a tourist when she's still missing.'

Tony smiled at her. 'You're a very loyal friend. Sara's lucky. But if you don't take some time off from looking for her, you'll go mad. We'll have to arrange for you to see Venice properly as well.'

They came to the alley leading to the Palazzo Berini and Petra's footsteps involuntarily slowed as they approached the door. Tony looked at her quickly. 'You needn't come in with me if you don't want to, you know. I can manage alone.'

'He might not be there,' Petra pointed out, half hopefully.

'Actually I'm hoping he isn't,' Tony told her as he rang the bell. 'His housekeeper sounded as if she knew something and I'd rather like to have a word with her.'

'She wouldn't tell me anything,' Petra reminded him.

He gave a very masculine smile, half amusement and half condescension. 'I think I might get a bit more out of her. She'll be frightened at the thought of the Consulate questioning her.' There was the sound of someone coming and he turned away.

Maria opened the door and looked at Tony with a polite smile but her expression changed when she saw Petra behind him. '*Si*, Signor?'

Tony produced a card from his pocket and put it into her hand, at the same time stepping through the doorway. '*El Conte Berini, per favore.*'

Maria stepped back to give him room and Petra hopped in behind him. '*Momento,*' she muttered, giving Tony an uneasy look after reading his card, and left them in the hall while she went through into the main house.

'Looks as if our luck's in and the Count's at home,' Tony remarked.

Petra wasn't sure if it was lucky or not; she had no wish to meet Carlo Berini again and could imagine the scathing look he would give her when Tony asked him to again disprove her allegations.

The housekeeper was soon back again and showed them up to the Count's business room on the first floor. He was standing with his back to them, apparently absorbed in something that was happening on the canal, but he turned as Maria closed the door behind her. His eyes went first to Petra, travelling over her, and she was glad that this time she was wearing a clean skirt and blouse instead of her crumpled travelling clothes or the jeans and sweater of last night. He gave her his usual thin smile. 'Good morning, Signorina. Did I not say that it wasn't goodbye?' Petra didn't answer and he turned to Tony, glancing down first at the card in his hand. 'Good morning, Signor Reid.'

Tony nodded and said briskly, 'I'm sorry to bother you, Count Berini, but . . .'

'Not at all. I have been expecting you,' the Count interposed, which completely threw Tony for a minute.

'Oh. Really?'

'Why yes. You see I was quite certain that Signorina Thornton didn't believe me when I said that I didn't know her friend, and as she is a very determined young lady, I guessed that she would go straight to the Consulate.'

'In that case you must know *why* I'm here,' Tony pointed out. 'I'm afraid we need more than just your word in this matter.'

'*Just* my word?' The Doges' descendant drew himself up to his full six foot three and Petra felt as if she'd shrunk to the size of a worm. But Tony stood up to him manfully.

'In this case, yes. I'm sure you understand. Something like this could lead to so many unsavoury rumours. Best to scotch them at the outset, don't you think?'

The Count's left eyebrow rose. 'Are you *threatening* me, Signor?'

'Good heavens, no.' Tony hastened to correct him. 'Just pointing out the possibilities, you know.'

To Petra's complete amazement, Berini threw back his head and laughed in genuine amusement. 'You're a brave man, Signor. One word in your Consul's ear and I could have you transferred to somewhere very cold and very unpleasant. But I happen,' his eyes moved to Petra, 'to admire your cause.'

Crossing to his desk he pulled open a drawer and took from it a largish envelope, which he tossed casually towards Tony. 'As I say, I was expecting your visit, so I had my secretary look out the bills you will find in that envelope. But knowing that Signorina Thornton is a very difficult lady to convince, I also sent someone to the passport office to retrieve this.' And he placed a leather-covered passport alongside the envelope on top of the desk.

Quickly Tony stepped forward and picked it up, flicking through the pages almost to the end, then he silently passed it, still open, to Petra. The date stamps were there quite clearly alongside the American visa. The Count had left Venice on the twenty-sixth of the previous month and had not returned until the tenth. She turned back to the beginning of the book and found that it was as he'd said, it was due to run out on the twenty-third. And it was most definitely his passport; his eyes seemed to be looking at her disdainfully from the photograph and could belong to no one else. He was, she noticed abstractedly, nearly thirty-one years old.

Tony had emptied the envelope on the table and was going rapidly through the papers inside. He turned to her and said, almost apologetically, 'These are all hotel, restaurant and car hire bills for the same period in America and also plane tickets in the Count's name. It will be easy to check but . . .'

'If you haven't already arranged to do so,' the Count put in sardonically.

Tony acknowledged the truth of that with a slight nod and said stiffly, 'Please accept my apologies. There can be no doubt that you were not the person who met Sara Hamling in Paris. But naturally we had to be sure.'

'Of course. You may take the papers with you if you wish to check them further.'

'I'm sure that won't be necessary.' Tony took the passport from Petra's slack fingers and put it back on the desk with the envelope. 'We won't trouble you any longer, Count. Thank you for your help.' He looked expectantly at Petra, waiting for her to add her apologies to his, but she was gazing blankly at the floor, her thoughts in turmoil. She had been so sure, so unshakeably certain that Sara was here that for the

moment she just couldn't take in all the implications. If
she wasn't here, then where? And if she hadn't gone
with Berini, then who had she gone with? Then came
the knowledge that she had made a complete fool of
herself and all for nothing.

'Petra,' Tony urged.

She turned obediently but swayed a little and put a
hand to her head.

'I think the Signorina is unwell,' Berini said sharply.
'A chair quickly.'

Petra found herself helped into a seat and then her
head was thrust firmly down between her knees. 'Take
deep breaths,' a voice commanded. Then, 'Ring for my
housekeeper and tell her to bring some smelling-salts.'

'No, I'm all right, really. Hey,' Petra protested when
she tried to straighten up and found her head still firmly
held down.

'You're not going to faint?'

'No.'

The Count took his hand from her head and she sat
up. 'I'm sorry. It was rather a shock, that's all.
Although it shouldn't have been. I mean, I should have
been glad that Sara hadn't been here, I suppose. But
now I don't . . .' She broke off, not really knowing what
she was trying to say, as the Count put a tall glass into
her hand. It was iced Perrier water and she sipped it
gratefully.

'Naturally it must have come as an unpleasant shock
to find that I am not a murderer, or even a seducer,'
Berini remarked with dry irony. 'I suppose you
imagined that I had become tired of your friend and
drowned her in the Grand Canal?'

The fact that she had been afraid of exactly that
brought a flush to Petra's cheeks and she gave him a
fiery look. He smiled, and for the first time the smile

reached his eyes, making him like a human being and not the ogre that she'd thought him. It was a pretty devastating smile too, and Petra wondered how on earth she'd ever been fool enough to suspect him.

'Er—I think I owe you an apology,' she began uncomfortably.

'You do,' he agreed. 'But it doesn't matter now. You're feeling better?' She nodded and he turned to Tony who was waiting nearby. 'Is there anything you can do to help find her friend?'

Tony shrugged rather helplessly. 'We'll try everything we can, of course. But if she didn't come here . . .' He left the sentence hanging.

'Then she could be anywhere,' Petra said dismally. 'I know. I don't have a clue where to start looking now.'

Coming over to her, Tony put a hand on her shoulder. 'Don't worry, we'll think of something. Come on, I'll walk you back to your digs.'

Petra got to her feet, but the Count said, 'One moment. I would like the Signorina to stay a little longer, if she will. I have already promised her my help in finding Signorina Hamling, but there are one or two points on which I'm not quite clear.'

'Thank you, Count Berini, but there's really no need for you to bother,' Tony told him formally. 'The Consulate will do everything in its power, you can be sure of that. And we've already taken up too much of your time.'

He moved to draw Petra towards the door but had hardly taken more than a step before Berini stopped him by saying. 'You seem to forget, Signor, that my name is involved in this matter. Even if Signorina Thornton refuses my help, I shall still pursue it. I do not like having my name used to seduce young girls. If this man, whoever he is, does so successfully once, then

he may do so again. And I might not be able to
establish my innocence so easily a second time. And I
think the only thing we can do is to start looking in
Venice as he seems so familiar with the city. But
perhaps we should let the lady herself decide.' He
turned to Petra. 'Will you accept my help, Signorina?'

'Of course I'll accept your help. I'll accept any help I
can get.' She turned towards Tony. 'I know you'll do all
you can, but you said yourself that the Count was a
powerful man in Venice; he may be able to get things
moving even more quickly than you can.'

'Then you'll stay and go through the whole thing
with me once more?' Berini pursued.

Petra nodded. 'Thanks for coming, Tony. When will
it be okay for me to call at the Consulate again?'

'Come any time you want. Here, I'll give you my
card. And I'll put my private telehone number on it in
case you need to get hold of me in a hurry.' He handed
the card to Petra then nodded to the Count. 'Thanks
again for your help, Count. I'm sure you'll let the
Consulate know should you happen to stumble across
anything.' His tone implying that he definitely didn't
expect him to.

'Of course. I'll show you out.'

The two men left the room and Petra went over to
the window overlooking the Canal, fascinated by the
maze of traffic that continuously went not only up and
down but also zig-zagged across it, making it more
hazardous than any busy street in England. But, by
some miracle, all the craft seemed always able to avoid
each other, although there was a constant cacophony of
hooters and sirens.

She didn't hear the Count come back into the room
and turned with a start to find him just behind her
when he said, 'It's a view that one can never tire of.'

'No, I don't suppose you do. It must be wonderful to live here.'

He moved forward to join her at the window. 'Yes, most of the time. But even the most beautiful cities can become mundane, especially when they are full of tourists all the year and constantly flooded in winter.'

'It must be worse in the summer though, mustn't it?'

'Yes, but I generally manage to get away to my villa in Sicily then. But this year I have—business in Venice.'

By 'business' did he mean his fiancée? Petra wondered. There was a pause which she broke by saying awkwardly, 'Look, I know I didn't apologise properly, but I really am sorry for suspecting you and . . .'

He held up his hand. 'That really isn't necessary. You were right to be suspicious in the beginning, but I regret that you weren't able to accept my assurances.'

'Taking someone's word of honour has sort of gone out in England now,' Petra explained.

He laughed with rich amusement. 'Which is a polite way of saying that it went out with the Dark Ages. I'm sorry, we tend to live in the past in Venice, you know.'

Petra smiled with him and said impulsively, 'You speak awfully good English.'

'That's because I'm more English than Italian.' He hesitated a moment, then said, 'Come, I'll show you.' Leading her out of the room, he turned to the right, pushing open high ornate double doors at the end of the corridor which gave on to a long picture gallery. 'These are all my ancestors,' he told her with a casual wave of his hand towards the framed faces in lace and silk and glowing velvet. 'This portrait is of the first Count Berini,' he indicated a very small dark picture of a man in medieval clothes. 'And this is his grandson, who was one of the Doges of Venice. You see he is

painted in his robes with the distinctive headdress.' He
went on down the room, pointing out a woman who
was said to be a great beauty and a man who was killed
by pirates, until he stopped at the last two portraits.
'This is my grandfather, who died only about ten years
ago. Next to him is his wife, an English woman, as was
my mother. She came to Venice as a tourist, but in
those days tourists made much longer visits, often for
two or three months. Which gave my grandfather time
to court her and persuade her to marry him.'

Old Count Berini was very like his grandson; the
same high cheekbones and thin, sensuous mouth. 'Did
she take much persuading?' Petra asked lightly.

'I'm told she put up quite a resistance; she had an
independent spirit and wasn't ready for marriage. My
father, on the other hand, met my mother when he was
at college in England and they were engaged for two
years before they married. Falling in love with English
women is a habit we Berinis had,' he added with a
smile.

Petra noticed that he said had and remembered that
he was going to break the habit by marrying an Italian
girl.

'Your parents' portraits aren't here,' she observed.

'No, they are in the grand salon. Through here.' He
opened the doors at the far end of the gallery and led
her into a huge room, a small ballroom, that was the
most magnificent she'd seen in the palazzo—and that
was saying something! With a little gasp of wonder she
moved into the room and saw her reflection mirrored a
dozen times in the huge, gilded mirrors that decorated
the walls.

'Those are my parents, at the far end of the room.'

Petra went first to look at his mother, who looked a
very pretty English girl with her light brown hair and

soft complexion, but there was a distinct glint of humour in her eyes which her son definitely hadn't inherited. She looked next at his father but, strangely, the Count didn't resemble him so much as his grandfather. His father hadn't so much arrogance; he looked a gentler, kinder man. More English, like Tony Reid, she decided.

'They died when I was quite young,' the Count remarked. 'They were caught in a hotel fire. My mother was pregnant and unable to climb to safety and my father wouldn't leave her.'

'How dreadful!' Petra stared at him, appalled.

'It was a long time ago.'

But it was something you never got over, not that. Petra suddenly pictured him as a small boy being told that his parents were dead, that he'd never see them again. 'It must have been terrible for you.'

He turned to look at her and his mouth twisted mockingly. Raising his eyebrows, he said, 'Are you feeling sorry for me, Signorina?'

Petra stiffened; whatever pity the child had warranted, the grown man certainly didn't want now, especially from a comparative stranger who was just an unwanted intruder into his life. 'No, of course not,' she answered stiffly.

He didn't believe her and the thought obviously amused him, but he said, 'Why don't we sit down and you can tell me about the phone call that you said your friend made to you after she left Paris?'

He led the way to a blue silk-upholstered settee on carved cabriole legs that looked so delicate that Petra was afraid it wouldn't take her weight let alone the Count's as well.

'She rang a few days after she left and . . .'

'Can you remember the exact date?' he interrupted.

'It was the eighth, I think. At about seven in the morning. I was busy with breakfast and everything and the kids were yelling at one another so unfortunately I couldn't hear very well, but Sara said that this man, Carlo, had lied to her all along and that she was leaving and coming back to Paris that day.'

'Did she just say that she was leaving or that she was leaving Venice?' he asked sharply.

Petra frowned, trying to remember, then shook her head regretfully. 'There was so much else going on at the same time. I might have just *assumed* she said or meant Venice because that was where I thought she was. D'you see what I mean?'

'Yes. It's an easy thing to do of course. But it doesn't give us much help. I take it she didn't get in touch with you again?'

'No. When she didn't turn up at the flat where we worked in Paris, I went to Peter Dudley, who works in UNESCO and is a friend of my father's. He tried to trace her but couldn't so then I came here to look for her myself.'

'Could she have gone back to her home in England?'

'No, her parents retired recently and have gone to visit her married brother in Australia for six months. Their house has been let out to someone else while they're away.'

'Perhaps she is staying with other friends there?'

'I suppose that's a remote possibility, but we're so close that we mostly know the same people; but I did think of that so I gave Peter Dudley a list of friends which he's having checked. But I just know it won't do any good because Sara wouldn't go back to England without telling me, especially when she said she was coming back to Paris. Sara may be impetuous,' she explained, 'but she isn't wilfully uncaring, if you see what I mean.'

A flicker of amusement shone in his dark eyes but was quickly gone. 'How do you know each other so well?'

'Our mothers went to school together, and were such good friends that they bought houses almost next door to one another when they married. Sara and I were in and out of each other's home all the time; it was like belonging to two families really.'

'But you're not alike.' Petra looked at him questioningly and he went on, 'Sara is the type who goes with men, but you, I think, are not.'

Petra flushed and admitted reluctantly. 'She does tend to fall in love rather a lot.'

'Love?' His eyebrows rose.

'Well, she always thinks it's love, at first anyway. There's nothing cold-blooded about the way she feels. She's always sure that she's met *the* man at last.'

'There have been a lot of men in Sara's life, then?'

Petra frowned. 'Look, Count Berini, it's very kind of you to help me and all that, but I hardly think that Sara's sex life is any concern of yours,' she told him roundly.

He grinned, making him look suddenly much younger. 'As I was accused of being a part of her sex life, I think it concerns me quite closely. And my name is Carlo, by the way,' he added. 'But you already know that.'

'Yes.' Petra looked at him uncertainly, surprised by his familiarity and not knowing quite what to make of it.

'If we're going to work together I think we might as well adopt your English informality, don't you? After all you only met your friend from the Consulate today, and yet I heard you call him Tony. So I'm Carlo, and you are Petra,' he prompted. 'An English name I don't think I've heard of before.'

'My parents are incurable romantics. They went to Petra for their honeymoon. You know, the Rose Red City in Jordan that's supposed to be as old as time.'

She broke off, feeling that she was saying too much and he would think her a fool, but he merely said, 'Yes, I've heard of it. Have you been there yourself?'

'Good heavens, no. I don't have that kind of money. Although I'd love to go.'

'Maybe you'll get there one day.'

Petra laughed. 'I doubt that very much.'

He looked at her with renewed interest when she laughed and was about to say something when there was a knock on the door and the housekeeper came in. She spoke to the Count in Italian but Petra understood the words telephone and Signorina Francesca.

'Excuse me for a few moments.'

He left the room with Maria and Petra wondered a little devilishly what his fiancée's reaction would be to the news that he was helping to find Sara; if he even bothered to tell her about it. Perhaps it was of little real importance to him now that his name had been cleared, although he was being very kind considering the way she'd barged into his life. Petra looked round the sumptuous room, feeling rather amazed that she was there at all. But it was very comforting to know that she had both Tony Reid and Carlo Berini helping her. Carlo! Somehow she didn't think she'd ever get used to calling someone who owned all this by his Christian name.

He didn't keep her waiting very long, only a few minutes, and definitely not long enough for Petra to become accustomed to her surroundings. She stood up when he came back and said, 'I must be going.'

His eyebrows rose. 'You're not still afraid of me, are you?'

'No. No, of course not.'

'Then why are you so nervous?'

Impossible to tell him that his very presence made her feel unsettled, so she shrugged and gestured round the huge room. 'All this, I suppose. It's a bit—overwhelming.'

'You find it so?'

'Why, yes. Don't you ever feel as if you're living in a museum?' she blurted out impulsively.

Carlo looked surprised and she could have kicked herself for making such a gauche remark, but he said simply, 'It's my home; I've never really known anything else. Everything here is as familiar to me as the things in your home must be to you. One merely looks after the palazzo and keeps it in good repair to hand on to the next generation. I do for my descendants what my ancestors did for me.'

For fun, Petra had once tried to trace her family tree, but had only got as far back as her great-great grandparents before she lost them altogether, so she found it virtually impossible to visualise an ancestry going way back into history, and even more impossible to think of her descendants marching on into the future and benefiting from anything she had done in her lifetime. Obviously the Count had an entirely different feeling of family and life; but then he was partly Italian.

'Do you happen to have a photograph of Sara with you in Venice?' he asked her, reverting to the main topic and making Petra feel as if she had been put back in her place.

'Why yes, I do.'

'Perhaps you could let me have it? I will have some copies made and have them shown round at the station and airports in the hope that someone may remember seeing her.'

'Well yes of course, if you think it will help,' Petra agreed dubiously. 'But it's only a snapshot of us both taken last summer.'

'It can easily be enlarged, and the fact that it's a recent photo will be very helpful. Unless of course,' he added wryly as a thought struck him, 'your friend has cut her hair or dyed it since.'

Petra was indignant. 'Certainly not. Sara has gorgeous fair hair. She'd never dream of dying it.'

Carlo laughed and opened the door for her. 'Good, I'm pleased to hear it. Do you intend to continue to stay at the café I took you to last night? Then I will walk there with you now to collect the photo, if I may. The sooner we show it round the better, I think. It's already quite some time since Sara was supposed to have come to Venice, and so many tourists come here in summer that people will forget if we don't hurry.'

As he spoke, he led the way back through the gallery and down the marble staircase. Maria was in the hall, dusting one of the row of marble busts that lined it, and gave Petra a disapproving look when she saw that Carlo was going out with her. She said something to him and he answered shortly before they went out into the street.

The sun was high overhead, beating down on to the pavements that seemed to sizzle in the heat. The Count glanced down at her. 'Your skin is too pale for the midday sun; you must be careful not to get burnt.'

Petra looked rather ruefully down at her white arms. 'We weren't given enough time off in Paris to sunbathe.'

'You worked there as an au pair, I think you said?'

'Yes.' She looked at him with chin raised challengingly, guessing that he must class her on the same level as a servant, and rather resenting it.

'Did you enjoy the work?'

'No, I hated it,' she admitted candidly, only now that she was free realising just how much she had hated it. 'And Sara couldn't stand it either, which is probably why she was tempted to go away with—whoever it was.'

'Why did you dislike it so much?'

'Because they were such a rotten family. If they'd been nice we would probably have stayed on till the end of our six months.'

'Perhaps you should have worked for an Italian family.'

'Could you guarantee they would be nice?'

Carlo laughed. 'Not guarantee it, no, but I think you would have been happier.'

They had arrived at the café and moved towards the entrance just as Vasco was coming out with a tray full of cups of coffee. He jumped and nearly dropped the lot when he saw who she was with, then stepped hastily aside to let them pass, giving Carlo a clumsy bow as he did so. The Count gave him a speculative glance and said, 'Was that your fellow conspirator?'

Petra gave him an innocently puzzled look. 'Sorry?'

In return she got one of his thin smiles. 'Someone had to help you over the wall into the garden of the palazzo, and again ferry you out to my boat. And he looks young enough and susceptible enough to be persuaded by a pretty girl into doing what she wanted, however foolish.'

She opened her mouth to deny it, but found him looking straight at her, so flushed and looked away.

'Thank you,' he said in amusement. 'I would much rather you did not lie to me, even to protect that boy. And I have a feeling that you would not be very good at it.'

Petra sighed. 'You're right; I've always been rotten at telling lies, I get found out every time.'

He laughed and would have said something more, but Emilio came bustling up, somehow bowing obsequiously, smoothing his apron, curling his moustaches, shouting for Vasco, and offering Carlo anything he wanted, all at the same time.

Carlo accepted a cup of coffee and sat down at a table while Petra went through the kitchen and ran up to her room to get the snapshot. It was a colour photo of both Sara and herself taken in the garden at home on a hot summer day. Sara was wearing shorts and a sun top, while Petra was in a bikini, a shirt thrown loosely over her shoulders but blown back by a slight breeze so that it hid nothing of her slim young body. Petra looked at it uncertainly, only now remembering that neither of them had been wearing very much, and feeling rather reluctant to hand it over to the Count. If he thought that they were promiscuous before, then the photo would only add to that impression. Hurrying over to the dressing table, she looked through her make-up bag for a pair of scissors so that she could at least cut herself off, but then remembered with annoyance that they were packed away in her big suitcase that she'd left behind in the left luggage department at the railway station in Paris. Darn! She looked round rather wildly for something else that would do but didn't like to pry into the absent owner's drawers. She would just have to give the Count the complete snapshot. No, not the Count, Carlo; she must remember to think of him by that name and then perhaps she wouldn't feel quite so nervous of him. And she'd kept him waiting long enough.

Hurrying downstairs, she paused in the doorway leading from the kitchen to get her breath back and looked through into the café. Carlo was seated at a table, calmly drinking his coffee and smoking a cigarette, but he looked completely out of place in his lightweight, stone-coloured suit, among the tourists in their shorts and bright shirts, and the local men in their old dark working clothes. He must be hating every minute of it, she thought, and be silently cursing her for involving him in something that brought him to such a place. But nothing of it showed in his face as he stood up when she went towards him.

Stubbing out his cigarette, he took the photo, which she handed to him face down, and turned it over. His eyebrows rose a little, but he only nodded and put it into his pocket. 'I'll let you have it back as soon as I've had the copies made.'

'Er—could you cut me off before you do that please?' she asked uncomfortably.

Carlo's eyes flashed with laughter, but he said gravely, 'Of course.' He reached for his wallet to pay for the coffee but Emilio came up and waved the money away, spouting out a whole stream of Italian. Carlo shook hands with her and said, 'I'll be in touch with you soon,' then let Emilio usher him outside, everyone in the café watching avidly and wondering who on earth he was. When he'd gone they all turned to look at Petra and then began to wonder who *she* was, their eyes wildly speculative. She turned and fled.

It was too early to hear anything from either of her helpers that day so Petra took the opportunity to do a little sightseeing in the afternoon, but Venice was hot and crowded, and her eyes were constantly searching the streets for a girl with long fair hair, so she didn't enjoy it as much as she would ordinarily have done. She kept wishing that Sara was there with her, sharing the city, as they had shared Rome and Paris and Vienna together in the past, ever since their first school trip abroad. It had never occurred to either of them to take a holiday apart and they knew each other so well that Petra could guess exactly what Sara's reactions would have been to every sight she saw: the Doge's palace with its Bridge of Sighs she would have liked, but St Marks's she would have found too much; she would have loved the Clock Tower, though, with its two larger than life Moorish figures, and gone crazy over the gondoliers in their striped shirts and beribboned straw hats. Had she been here? Had she seen these things? Petra stood on a bridge over one of the lesser canals, leaning on the wall and looking down to the Grand Canal about thirty yards away, her thoughts on her friend, her mind distraught with worry.

Her stock at the café had risen considerably since Carlo had gone there with her and that evening Emilio gave her an even larger helping of pasta and chips. Petra ate what she could, but the next morning was still full and could hardly face the plate of fried eggs, bacon and sausage that Emilio proudly placed in front of her.

'Is the English breakfast,' Vasco translated for him. 'He know all the English; they love the big breakfast.'

Petra looked at the heap of food, greasy from having been fried in too much oil, and heaved. 'Could—could I eat it outside, please?'

'Of course. Of course.' They set her a place at one of the outside tables and one of the local dogs got the best surprise of his life when he was fed large portions of her breakfast whenever no one was looking. Vasco and Emilio both exclaimed with pleasure at her empty plate and Emilio wanted to give her another helping which she hastily and firmly refused.

Before she'd really had time to work out what she was going to do that day, Emilio called her to the phone and she lifted the receiver in excited anticipation. 'Hallo. This is Petra Thornton.'

'Morning Petra. It's Tony.'

'Have you found out something?' she asked eagerly, sure that his call must mean good news.

But Tony only laughed ruefully. ''Fraid not. Miracles take us a bit longer, you know. How are you this morning?'

'Oh, fine thanks.'

'You weren't eaten by the lion, then, after I left you alone with him yesterday?'

'By Carlo?' Petra hadn't thought of him as a lion, he reminded her more of a bird of prey, of an eagle, or one of the hawks on the mooring posts at his door. 'No, he was okay.'

'Listen, if you're not doing anything this morning, how about having coffee with me later on? I can get away to meet you at about eleven, if that's okay?'

'Yes, that's fine. Where shall I meet you?'

He told her how to get to a coffee shop in a square near the Consulate, then added, 'And if you have a photo of Sara, could you bring it with you? It might help.'

'I'm sorry, Tony, but Count Berini's borrowed the only photograph I had with me. You must both have had the same idea.' But Carlo had it first, Petra thought with annoyance, wishing that it had been Tony. 'But he promised to give it back to me as soon as he'd had it copied.'

'We'll have to wait, then. Not to worry, it might hold things up a little, that's all. See you at eleven.'

Petra spent the couple of hours in between in just wandering round the city looking for Sara. Once she thought she saw her some way ahead and ran through the narrow streets, pushing people aside, afraid that the girl might turn into a side alley and be lost. But when she came close and shouted, 'Sara, Sara,' the blonde girl didn't turn round, and Petra knew even before she came up to her and grabbed her arm that she'd got the wrong person. It turned out to be a Scandinavian girl with her boyfriend, blonder than Sara close to, and with a much bigger bust measurement. Luckily the girl was very nice about being grabbed so fiercely, but Petra walked away feeling foolish. And Sara wouldn't have been at all pleased at being mistaken for the bigger girl, Petra thought, picturing her friend's reaction with a grin. Then silly tears pricked her eyes and she had to blink hard to drive them away. Crying wasn't going to help; she had to think positive. Taking out her map, Petra strode towards her rendezvous with Tony.

She was there before him and was halfway down a long cold drink before he hurried in, looking hot and rather out of breath. 'Phew, I'm looking forward to this drink.' He pulled his tie loose and took it off, looking enviously at her sun-top and shorts. 'Lord, what I wouldn't give to be able to dress like that in this heat, but suits are *de rigueur* in the British Foreign Service.'

'Isn't your building air-conditioned?'

'Oh, sure, but it's when you go outside that it hits you. What's that you're drinking? Would you like another one?'

'Yes, please. It's pressed orange juice.'

Tony beckoned the waiter over and ordered the drinks, but Petra couldn't wait till they came to ask, 'Still no news?'

'Sorry, no. But we're pulling all the stops out and

ordering a full-scale search. All the borders between Italy and England have been asked to look out for Sara and we've done the same at the Austrian border as well just in case. We've also contacted the police and asked them to check all the hospitals in the remote chance that she might have hitch-hiked and been involved in an accident and be lying unconscious in a hospital somewhere. Not that that's at all likely,' he added quickly when he saw Petra's face pale.

'No, no of course not.' She resolutely pushed that picture out of her mind. 'Have you been in contact with Peter Dudley? Has he managed to check that list of friends I gave him yet?'

'We have and he has. But no joy, I'm afraid. None of the people on your list have seen Sara since you left for Paris and none of them have received more than a postcard—most of them written by you, it seems—and definitely no word within the last month.'

'Sara always did hate writing letters,' Petra said dismally. 'We're back to square one again, then?'

'No, because before we were concentrating just on Venice, but now we're looking for her over half of Europe.'

'Wow!' But somehow the thought of hundreds of people out there looking for Sara brought little comfort. 'Don't you think Carlo Berini was right, then, to keep looking in Venice?'

Tony shrugged. 'He keeps a flat in Paris and a chalet in Switzerland, also he goes to America and the Bahamas a lot and spends holidays in the South of France. Someone could have met him, or even seen him, in any of those places and decided to use his name. At the moment we're trying to find out if a similar thing has happened before. We've got Interpol on to that,' he added quietly.

Petra stared at him, really impressed, and feeling
suddenly frightened by what she'd started. God, what if
Sara was perfectly safe somewhere? Wonderful, of
course, but how on earth would she ever start to
apologise for sending what sounded like half the police
forces of Europe on a wild goose chase?

Tony mistook her reaction and put a comforting
hand over hers. 'Try not to worry; I'm sure she'll turn
up safe and sound.'

Petra gulped, and was grateful to be able to lower her
head and concentrate on her drink.

'Now,' Tony said briskly, removing his hand. 'I've
a couple of questions I've been told to ask you.' But
he more or less went over the whole thing again with
her, making notes, and covering much the same
ground as she'd gone into with Carlo yesterday.
'Good.' Half an hour later Tony slipped his notepad
back into his pocket and grinned at her. 'Let's talk
about you now. Can you stay on in Venice for a
while?'

'Yes, of course. For as long as it takes.'

'Have you got enough money? Sorry to be blunt, but
it's best to come right out and ask.'

'I've got enough for about four weeks, five if I'm very
careful. After that I'll have to ask my parents for some,
because my savings are mostly in a deposit account at
home, but they'll let me borrow against it until I go
back to England.'

'Good, that's okay, then.' Neither of them voiced
the thought that was uppermost in their minds at that
moment; that they might never find Sara, or else find
her in tragic circumstances. 'Next question: what are
you doing on Saturday?'

'Why—nothing.' Petra was completely thrown.

'Then how about spending the day over at the Lido

with me and then having dinner back here in Venice in the evening?'

Petra smiled at him. 'You're not taking pity on me, are you?'

Tony grinned back, his eyes openly admiring. 'I rather hope it will be the other way around.'

She laughed and said, 'I'd love to. I can't wait to get a tan. I'm much too white.' She remembered Carlo saying that her skin was pale and wondered why she'd thought of him now.

'Great. I expect I'll be in touch with you before then so we can make arrangements to meet nearer the time.' Leaning forward, Tony said earnestly, 'Look, don't get me wrong; I know from your point of view it's a hell of a way to meet anyone, but from mine—well, I'm glad that you had to come to the Consulate, although I'm sorry about Sara, if you understand what I'm trying to get at.'

'Of course I do. And thanks. It's a great comfort to know that you're helping me.' He looked a bit wry at that so she laughed. 'And I'm glad I met you, too.'

He put his hand over hers again, but not in reassurance this time. 'I'd like to have asked you to have dinner with me before Saturday, but unfortunately our Ambassador to Italy is coming to Venice for a few days so I've got to meet him at the airport tonight and then there are official receptions tomorrow and the following day, so Saturday's the first free day I can manage.' He glanced ruefully at his watch. 'And now I'm afraid I have to get back; we're having a meeting over lunch to sort out the last details of H.E.'s visit.'

'H.E.?'

Tony grinned. 'Sorry. His Excellency the Ambassador.' He put some money on the table for their drinks and walked her out into the sun. 'Sorry I have to go.

Saturday seems a long way off, but I'll phone you before then. *Ciao!*

He hurried away, picking his way surely through the crowds and Petra envied him his knowledge of the city and his way of life. For all he made it sound like a duty, it must be fun to move among the powerful and famous, to go to diplomatic parties, and to have the opportunity of rising really high himself someday. She was glad he had asked her out; she already liked him and felt that in time she could possibly like him much more.

CHAPTER FIVE

THE next day was pretty empty, bringing only a note from Carlo, delivered by hand to the café, and containing her original snapshot and a blow up picture of just Sara's head and shoulders. It was a good enlargement showing clearly Sara's vivacious features, from her arched eyebrows to laughing mouth. Quickly, before worry could get to her again, Petra picked up the note that went with it. It was typed on thick white notepaper with a crest at the top, and read, 'I return your photograph together with one of the copies. I'm sure it will be of help but it is too soon yet for any results.' Then there were Carlo's initials at the bottom in thick black ink.

Petra held the note for several minutes, wondering who had typed it for him. He had mentioned a secretary before when she'd gone to see him with Tony, and Petra tried to imagine his secretary. Definitely female, she decided at once, and picked for her efficiency rather than her looks; but she would be good-looking too— the Count could afford to pick and choose—probably a young dark-haired Italian girl whose slimness was just verging on the voluptuousness that Italian woman are famous for. Glancing in the ornate mirror on the wall, Petra caught sight of her own almost boyishly slim figure and threw the note down on the floor. Yeuk! What the hell did it matter to her what Carlo's secretary looked like anyway? If he wanted a woman he could get one anywhere; he didn't have to have one on hand at his office as well. Angry with herself for even thinking about it. Petra put the enlargement of Sara in her bag and took it round to the Consulate to be passed on to Tony.

It wasn't until Petra got back and saw the note lying on the floor that she realised it had been delivered by hand and wondered if Carlo had brought it himself, then decided that that was unlikely and that he'd probably have given it to his secretary or housekeeper to deliver. Thinking about Maria made Petra remember how scared the housekeeper had seemed when she had tried to talk to her in the market. Why had she been so scared? Did she know something about Sara that Carlo didn't? After all, she was presumably a live-in housekeeper and must have been in the palazzo while he was away.

The thought excited her so that Petra impulsively grabbed her bag and hurried out again, taking the now familiar route to the Palazzo Berini. A glance from the end of the alleyway into the Canal showed that Carlo's boat was tied up at the steps, and Petra went back to confidently knock on the door.

It was a few minutes before Maria answered and she frowned when she saw who it was. Petra, determined to find out why she had that effect on the woman, said, 'Count Berini, please,' and moved to step inside, but the older woman barred her way.

'El Conte is not at home.'

Taken aback, Petra blurted, 'But his boat is there, I saw it.'

'El Conte is not at home,' Maria repeated and began to shut the door.

'Then I'll wait. Hey! Ouch!' She hastily stuck a foot in the doorway and got it squashed.

'You go. El Conte not see you.' Maria tried to push the door shut as Petra struggled to keep it open.

'Wait a minute. He will see me if you ask him,' Petra panted, her shoulder against the door.

A sharp voice from inside spoke in Italian and the pressure against the door was suddenly withdrawn so that it flew open and Petra almost fell into the hall, her bag flying from her hand. She managed to recover her balance but not her dignity, especially when she saw Carlo's fiancée looking over his shoulder as he stood in the doorway of one of the downstairs rooms, a frown creasing his brows.

The frown changed to a look of surprise when he saw her. 'Petra?' Stepping forward, he picked up her bag and gave it to her. 'Has something happened?'

'No.' Petra shook her head uncomfortably, deeply aware of the casualness of her faded denim shorts and sun top against the cool elegance of his fiancée. 'I wanted to ask you about something.'

'I see.' He frowned again but gestured towards the door he'd come out of. 'You'd better come in here.'

He said something else to the housekeeper, then closed the door. Turning to his girlfriend, Carlo said, 'This is Signorina Thornton from England. She is in Venice to look for a friend of hers who has disappeared, and I am helping to try to find her. And this is Signorina Francesca Canova,' he added to Petra, but obviously didn't think it necessary to give her any explanation of who the other woman was.

'But this is the girl who was in your garden,' Francesca exclaimed in fluent English that made Petra feel even more gauche and uneducated.

'*Sì.* What is it you wanted to ask me?'

'Well, it's—look, I'm sorry, I didn't mean to intrude when you're with your—er—guest. I'll come back some other time.' Petra backed awkwardly towards the door. 'If you could just tell me when you'll be free.'

'Since you are here, you may as well ask me now,' Carlo pointed out brusquely. 'After all, you must have thought it important to insist on seeing me.'

Petra flushed; it had seemed very important at the time, but now she was beginning to feel a complete fool. And she hated the way Francesca kept looking at her as if she was some kind of freak. 'No, honestly, it can wait.' She reached for the door handle.

'Petra,' Carlo said harshly, 'just say what you came to say. You needn't be afraid of speaking in front of Signorina Canova, if that's what's worrying you; I was about to tell her about you myself.'

'Well, okay.' Petra nodded, but her voice was still uncertain as she said, 'It's about your housekeeper. I tried to talk to her the day after I saw you for the first time, but she wouldn't answer any of my questions about Sara, and she—well, she seemed really scared. As if she was afraid of me.'

'And?' Carlo prompted.

'Well, it occurred to me that she was here in the house all the time you were away and that she might know something.'

'What kind of thing might she know?'

'I haven't the faintest idea,' Petra answered shortly. 'But she was here, she's scared and she won't answer my questions.'

Carlo looked at the stress in her face and said more gently, 'I'm afraid you're clutching at straws—is that the correct expression? Maria wasn't at the palazzo while I was in America. I gave her permission to go and visit her married sister who lives in Venice Mestre and who has been ill lately. And it is quite possible that she did not answer your questions simply because she didn't understand them. Her English isn't very good, you know.'

'But that doesn't explain why she was so afraid of me,' Petra pointed out, but already aware that she was fighting a losing battle.

'No, it doesn't. But you are rather a—determined young lady. It may be that Maria was afraid of the forceful way you approached her. She was attacked by some youths recently and her handbag taken.'

'I see.' Petra bit her lip. 'I'm sorry I've wasted your time. I obviously shouldn't have come here.'

'Oh, but you should,' Carlo disagreed. 'Any idea, anything that you think might help, I should like to know of it. And yours would have been a good idea if Maria had been here at the time. But even so, I will certainly talk to her myself. She took her own keys to the palazzo with her when she went and it's possible that she came back once or twice while I was away to dust or something.' He waved a hand in a gesture that betrayed a complete lack of knowledge about such mundane domestic chores.

'She could have come back?' Petra was immediately eager again. 'Then she might have seen something. You'll ask her?'

'Of course. But not now.' He put a familiar hand under Francesca's elbow. 'We were just about to have coffee in the drawing-room. Come and join us.'

'Oh no, I'd rather not, thanks.'

'But you must,' Francesca broke in. 'I am fascinated to know what this is all about. Tell her she must stay, Carlo.' She pouted a little and moved closer to him.

'You see, Signorina Canova is longing to hear your story. And I'm sure you would enjoy a cup of Maria's coffee.'

He opened the door for them both and Petra reluctantly followed Francesca into the chandelier-hung blue-and-white drawing-room. The coffee tray had

already been placed on a low table and Francesca
automatically went to sit in front of it, her role as
future mistress of the palazzo coming quite naturally
to her.

'Ring for another cup, Carlo. Do sit down,
Signorina—Thornton, was it not?' She waved her
hand gracefully towards a chair, her English with an
Italian accent attractive. 'I expect you are like all
English people and like milk and sugar with your
coffee?'

'Thank you, but I prefer it black,' Petra replied and
tried to hide a grimace as she took her first sip and
found it far more bitter than she'd expected.

'Is it not to your liking?' Francesca asked.

'No, it's fine, just rather hot,' Petra lied, then
remembered that Carlo had once said that she didn't
tell lies very well and gave him a quick glance under her
lashes. He was taking a cup from Francesca and not
looking at her, but there was an amused twist at the
corner of his handsome mouth. Damn him, Petra
thought angrily, and wished she hadn't been coerced
into staying.

'Now, you must tell me all about this mystery
concerning Maria and your friend. Does Maria know
her?' Francesca asked, settling back against the blue silk
settee that was a perfect foil for her pale green dress.
Carlo began to explain, still speaking English for
Petra's benefit, and Francesca gave him all her
attention except for one or two startled looks in Petra's
direction when she heard that Sara had been picked up
in a nightclub and that they had actually been working
as au pairs. Petra watched them both, only half
listening. They would make a handsome couple, both
dark and sophisticated and with the confidence that
comes with great wealth. Francesca was as nearly

beautiful as made no difference and she knew how to
make the best of herself, wearing a pleated skirt to
make her hips look slimmer and showing off her legs by
crossing them at the ankles. Petra wondered what she
would look like in ten or fifteen years time and
uncharitably hoped that she would be fat and double-
chinned. But she probably wouldn't be; she was rich
enough to pay to keep thin.

Petra's eyes turned to Carlo, able to watch him freely
as he talked to the other girl. He was too good looking
for her taste, she decided, only the hardness of his face
detracting from his handsomeness, if it could be called a
detraction, many would think quite the opposite. And
he was probably much too handsome for his own good,
especially being wealthy as well. He was probably a
playboy, or had been when he was younger, before he
decided to settle down with Francesca. There was a hint
of sensuality about his mouth that just might betray a
sexually passionate nature, and she guessed that he
must be very experienced. It occurred to her, though,
that they didn't behave like lovers, or at least Carlo
didn't. Apart from putting his hand under Francesca's
elbow that one time, he had made no attempt to touch
her, even when she'd moved close to him. Perhaps
upper class Italians didn't show their emotions, Petra
hazarded. Or perhaps they weren't in love, and it was to
be a marriage of mutual convenience, a joining of
financial and family interests. She could certainly sense
none of the strong excitement that rippled just under
the surface among other friends who'd been in love. Or
even the tension that existed when a couple were
physically attracted but hadn't yet been to bed together.
Petra couldn't begin to guess whether Carlo and
Francesca had slept together, perhaps they'd already
made love so many times that it had become

commonplace and they were like an older married couple, their initial passions all burnt out.

Carlo brought the story up to date, setting down his coffee cup and glancing at Petra as he did so. Something of her thoughts must have shown for his brows rose, an arrested expression on his face. Petra's hazel eyes met his dark ones for a sizzling moment before she quickly looked away, schooling her features into social blandness, but her heart beating just a little bit faster.

'I do hope you find your friend soon, Signorina,' Francesca was saying. 'But if she is in the habit of going alone to nightclubs ...' She shrugged eloquently. 'Would you like another cup of coffee?'

Petra could have thrown the pot at her; the implication that Sara was promiscuous couldn't have been more explicitly stated if she had put it into words of one syllable. 'Yes, Sara is very popular,' Petra said tightly. 'But then *she's* very fair and very beautiful. As tall, fair girls so often are, aren't they?' she added for good measure before standing up and putting her coffee cup back on the tray. 'Thank you so much for the coffee,' she said to Carlo. 'Perhaps you'll let me know when you've talked to Maria?'

'Of course. I'll see you out.'

After she had said a stiff goodbye to Francesca, he walked her through the house to the street door. Petra turned to say goodbye but before she could do so Carlo picked up her hand and examined the back of it.

'Hmm, surprising.' He ran a finger along the edge of her neatly cut and manicured nails.

'What is?'

'I quite expected your nails to be longer and sharper. Most cats have sharp claws, don't they?'

Petra flushed, knowing exactly what he meant, and

he still had hold of her hand, which didn't help. 'Sorry,' she apologised, but didn't really mean it.

Carlo looked at her reflectively. 'You always defend your friend very loyally.'

'Sara would do the same for me.'

'But I doubt if she would have to. Please, don't be angry. I admire your loyalty. You're a good person to have as a friend.'

'Thanks. It's nice of you to say so. Look,' she went on awkwardly, 'I'm truly sorry if I've offended your fiancée. Please apologise to her from me.'

He grinned. 'Certainly not. Didn't you see Francesca's nails? They're much longer and sharper than yours. And where do you get the idea that she's my fiancée? That's the second time you've called her that.'

'You mean she isn't?'

'No, she is merely an old family friend.'

'Oh, I see. I just—sort of gathered that you were engaged. Someone said that it was about time you got married and that you'd got a girl, and I just thought . . .' She broke off, aware that she was talking too much again and wishing that Carlo didn't make her nervous all the time.

His eyes were alight with amusement. 'So the people of the café think it's time I was married, do they? Well, maybe they're right at that. Perhaps I'd better come along and ask them who they think would make me a suitable wife.'

Petra's heart skipped a beat at the thought that she'd got Vasco into trouble, but then she realised that Carlo was teasing her and laughed nervously in relief. Raising her hand, he kissed it lightly. 'Goodbye Petra, and try to stop worrying quite so much. If Sara is in Venice I will find her, and if she has been here I will find out about it and learn where she's gone to.'

Her head felt somewhat dazed as she walked away; her hand had been kissed by a real live Italian Count—no Venetian Count, that meant much more. She hadn't thought that men still did that! But it had only been in fun, because he was teasing her. Carlo was different when he was teasing, more on her level somehow, but he still made her feel self-conscious, and she rather resented the fact that he seemed to find her so amusing.

It was interesting that he wasn't actually engaged to Francesca, though. Petra wondered why he'd bothered to tell her. In case she met the other girl again and made some embarrassing remark, presumably. Which meant he thought it possible they might meet a second time, no, third if you counted the time in the garden. Obviously the other girl was at the palazzo quite a lot. So maybe they did go to bed together after all. There had been a possessiveness about Francesca's attitude that betrayed some kind of relationship; maybe she was working on Carlo to propose to her by demonstrating what a good mistress of the palazzo she'd make—as well as being a good mistress in bed.

Petra pushed the strangely disturbing thoughts out of her mind. It was nothing to her who Carlo went to bed with—just so long as he'd never slept with Sara.

It was impossible to forget her worry over Sara completely, but Petra came close to it several times on her day out with Tony. They took the vaporetto over to the Lido, a seven-mile long strip of flat land that was really little more than large sand bars separating the lagoon from the Adriatic sea. Most of it had been taken over by hotels, but Tony was an old hand and found them an area of beach that wasn't too crowded. They spread their towels out on the sand and undressed,

Tony down to a pair of swimming trunks, Petra taking off her shorts and top to reveal a pale green bikini.

Tony looked up at her admiringly as she gathered up her hair and clipped it up on her head so that her back could get brown. 'Don't you burn with your colouring?'

'No, I'm lucky, I go brown straight away.' Petra stretched out beside him on her towel, enjoying the way he looked at her. She had hardly had a date in the three months since she came to Europe and it was nice to know that she was still a girl and still attractive. Definitely so if the look in Tony's eyes was anything to go by.

He smiled at her. 'You *are* lucky. I go bright lobster pink and peel a couple of times before I really start to tan.'

'But you're brown now.'

'That's because I've been coming over here every time I've had a day off since the beginning of the summer. You've missed all the red stages.'

'What a pity, I always wanted to go out with a Red Indian,' Petra teased. He laughed and made to give her a playful punch on the jaw, and then, when she asked him, told her all about his life in the Diplomatic Corps. He had travelled a lot even though he was so young, being moved on by the Foreign Office every couple of years or so. He understated his job, making it appear commonplace and even dull, but Petra was sure it wasn't.

'It must surely be exciting at times,' she said rather wistfully.

'It has moments when it's pretty hectic,' he admitted. 'But most of the time it's just sitting at a desk doing paperwork, like any other office.'

'But what about all those diplomatic parties and receptions; surely you find those exciting?'

'At first I did, but it was mostly because it was all so new and I was nervous, but after the first five dozen or so you start to get a bit blasé, and then they become just part of the job and often a nuisance when you'd rather be at home having a quiet read—or taking out a girl you've just met and would very much rather be with,' he added, reaching out to gently lift a curl from her neck with his finger.

Petra smiled but refused to get serious. 'I bet you say that to all the girls who come to you for help?'

Tony gave her a mock leer. 'I have an arrangement with the front office that they only send the best-looking ones in to see me.'

Petra played along, raising her eyebrows and saying, 'You have *that* much influence, huh?'

'Well actually,' he leaned closer to whisper in her ear, 'it cost me most of my salary every month to bribe them until I hit on the idea of telling them that there was a beautiful spy on the loose so if any gorgeous girls came into the Consulate they were to send them in to me at once.'

She burst out laughing. 'And how many beautiful spies have you had to deal with?'

'At least six a day,' he answered complacently. 'If I get less than five I feel absolutely cheated.'

'You're crazy.' Sitting up, Petra reached into her bag for some sun-tan oil, then hesitated. 'Are we going for a swim?'

'We can chance it if you like, but it's pretty mawky.'

They chanced it anyway, and spent the rest of the day swimming and sunbathing, apart from having a snack lunch and taking a walk along the beach. The sand was so hot that you couldn't walk on it with bare feet so they made use of the wooden duckboard-ing that stretched along the length of the beach, but this was so crowded with people that they made only slow progress. The sea, too, seemed to be full, not only with swimmers, but with dinghys, sailing boats and, further out, speed-boats that seemed to be constantly racing one another.

'Is it always this crowded?' Petra asked, rather overpowered. 'There must be miles of this beach and yet it's all full of people.'

'There are seven miles of it. But the big hotels take up most of it, so there isn't much left for people who come out from the city, I'm afraid. A bit like Blackpool in the height of the season, isn't it?' he said ruefully.

Petra touched his arm. 'It's probably pouring with rain in Blackpool right now, but this heat is gorgeous. I've been dying to sunbathe for ages. Thanks for bringing me, Tony.'

He put an arm lightly round her waist and drew her nearer. 'The pleasure's all mine. Especially when you're wearing that.' He nodded towards her bikini.

His arm was hot on her skin but Petra didn't try to draw away. She hadn't known him long of course but he wasn't trying to push it, and she rather liked to feel the strength and warmth of his arm and all that it implied.

In the evening they took a water-taxi back to the city, sharing it with several other people who had also opted out of queuing and fighting their way on the jam-packed vaporettos. Then Tony led her away from the busy streets around St Marco and took her to a restaurant near the Rialto Bridge where they sat at an outside table on the edge of the canal, watching the lights gradually come on all along the banks of the waterway and on the hundreds of boats and gondolas that used it.

'It's a very romantic city, isn't it?' Petra said with a

small sigh as she looked at the floodlit bridge. 'Even more romantic than Paris.'

'I know several people who would disagree with you, but I see what you mean.' Tony looked at her keenly. 'You're wishing you were here in other circumstances, aren't you?'

'Yes. Sorry.'

'No, I wish the same thing. But at least I'm glad that I'm trying to help.'

Petra leaned forward, her hands resting on the table. 'Just being here with you, and having today—that's helped too. More than you realise.'

'Good.' Tony picked up her hand and held it. 'I hoped it might.' He paused, then said with difficulty, 'Look, I've got to say this, Petra. I should have done when I first met you, but I didn't want our—friendship to start that way. You must be prepared for the worst; for not finding her or for . . . well, I don't have to spell it out to you, do I? Sorry to say it now, but it has to be said.'

'Yes, I know.' Petra looked down at her hand lying in his as she felt it begin to shake until Tony held it more tightly. 'I think that with every day that goes by and there's still nothing . . . I think I become more prepared for the worst and yet—somehow less.' She raised troubled eyes to his. 'Is there so little hope, then? Carlo Berini seems confident that we'll find a trace of her if she came to Venice.'

Tony shrugged, dismissing Carlo. 'I think he's only really offering token help because he feels he ought to as he's been involved. And there's nothing that he can do that we can't. All he can do at the most is to duplicate what we're doing.'

'But he's a native Venetian. Surely that counts for something? He must have loads of contacts—in Europe as well.'

'Among people of his own standing and interest, yes. But we need to search among ordinary people: train inspectors, border guards, ticket sellers at the Doge's Palace or the Campanile, that kind of person. Can you see Berini ever going near someone like that, let alone having contacts among them?'

'No, I suppose not,' Petra admitted doubtfully. 'But surely Carlo could find someone who could ask the questions for him?'

'And so can we. That's just what I'm saying: he personally can't do any more than we can.' His hand loosened. 'You called him Carlo. You surely don't call him that to his face?'

'What?' Petra was still thinking about what he'd said. 'Well, yes, I suppose I do.' She saw Tony's surprise and added, 'He asked me to.'

'You surprise me. I'd never have thought him that—casual.'

'Well, he heard me calling you Tony and said that we might as well be as informal as the English. He's as English as he is Italian, you know. Maybe he'll call you Tony if you see him again,' she went on lightly.

'Humph.' He gave a snorting kind of laugh. 'I very much doubt it. His kind don't get on familiar terms with lowly Consular officials.'

'But he can't be much older than you?'

'Age has nothing to do with it, it's position. He had his given to him on a plate the minute he was born, I'm having to work for mine.' Petra thought for a second that there was a trace of resentment in his voice, but then Tony leaned forward and smiled at her, holding her hand in both his. 'I'm probably doing him an injustice. I expect he told you to call him Carlo to put you more at ease. Any anyway I much prefer my position to his, especially when I'm sitting here in the moonlight, listening to the sound of violins from across the water and holding the hand of a beautiful girl.'

'You know, Tony, I think you're a romantic,' she teased.

'Definitely,' he agreed emphatically. 'romance was just what I had in mind.'

Petra gurgled with laughter. 'That isn't what I meant at all.'

And their conversation became light-hearted and playful again.

It was long past midnight when Tony walked her home, making their way carefully through the litter in the courtyard to the back door of the café.

'Good night,' Petra whispered. 'Thank you for a wonderful day. It was just what I needed.'

'Glad to oblige.' Tony put his hands on her waist and pulled her nearer. 'I'm duty officer tomorrow but perhaps you'll have dinner with me again soon?' Leaning forward he kissed her lightly on the cheek and then gently moved round to her mouth. It was a nice kiss, warm and undemanding, and Petra liked it.

'Yes, all right,' she agreed, and let him kiss her again.

'I don't want to leave you,' Tony murmured, his cheek against hers. 'This feels—so right.'

Petra pulled away a little and smiled at him. 'I'm so glad I met you, Tony.'

'That definitely calls for another kiss.' He pulled her closer, his body against hers and kissed her lingeringly. 'I'll phone you tomorrow.'

'Okay. Good night.' Petra parted from him reluctantly and climbed the long flights of stairs in a pleasantly sleepy haze. Tony was really nice, and she could easily get used to having him around.

The next couple of days passed without Petra seeing either of her two helpers, but Tony did ring and he also sent round her snapshot of Sara. With nothing better to do, Petra wandered round the city herself, showing the photograph and asking gondoliers, shopkeepers, café waiters, anyone she thought might be able to help and could speak some English, if they had seen the other woman. One or two looked at it a little longer, so that her hopes were raised, but in the end they, as well as everybody else, shook their heads, usually adding, 'There are so many in Venice. So many young girls.'

Petra began to feel dispirited to say the least and only her youth and natural optimism kept her from being really depressed. She began to think seriously of trying to contact Sara's parents in Australia and decided to discuss it with Tony that evening when he had again asked her out to dinner. But when she returned to the café from another fruitless trek round the simmeringly hot city, looking forward to a bath and meeting Tony, Vasco greeted her eagerly and put a note into her hands. It was from Carlo, but written in his own hand this time, strong writing that cared little for economy of paper yet which didn't waste words. 'I have some information for you. I'll call for you at seven-thirty this evening.'

The thought that he might have news of Sara lifted her to dizzy heights of hope and she ran excitedly upstairs, but then the basic awkwardness of the situation struck her. Now what am I supposed to do? Petra groaned in perplexity. Do I break my date with Tony to listen to what Carlo has to tell me, which might only take a short while, or do I keep my date with Tony and put off Carlo? But there was no question of the latter; however important this information of Carlo's was, she wanted to hear it straightaway. There was, of course, a third alternative: she could keep her date with Tony and they could see Carlo together, but somehow she shrank from that; although superficially polite, Petra sensed that neither man had really hit it off with the other. Tony definitely hadn't gone much on Carlo, and, although Carlo's feelings were kept under a stricter control and were less easy to define, he hadn't unbent at all towards Tony.

Going downstairs again, Petra used sign language to ask Emilio if she could use the phone and he gestured lavish permission; since they'd known she was an acquaintance of Carlo's nothing was too much trouble at the café. When she got through to Tony Petra explained apologetically and said, 'I feel that I really must meet him and learn what he's found out. It could be important.'

'If it was that important he would hardly have just left a note,' Tony pointed out rather sourly. 'And he should have come to us with any information he had, not kept it to himself.'

'He hasn't been in touch with you, then?'

'No. And even if he'd seen someone in higher authority here they would have passed the message on to me. Everyone knows I'm taking a special interest in this case.'

Petra felt a louse. 'I'm sorry, Tony,' she apologised again. 'But I feel that I really must meet him. Perhaps I could phone you at home after I've seen him?'

'It will be too late for the booking I've made by then. I think it would be best if I cancel it for tonight and make it for tomorrow instead. You can make it for tomorrow, I take it?' he added wryly.

'Yes, of course. I didn't want this, Tony. I was looking forward to tonight.'

'So was I. That's why I'm so fed up about it. Try and get rid of him as soon as you can and then give me a ring here; there's loads of work to catch up on and I may as well stay behind for a couple of hours. If he doesn't take too long we might still be able to get in somewhere for a meal, although you know how full all the restaurants in Venice get during the summer season.'

'Okay, I'll phone you as soon as I can.'

Petra put the phone down and went back upstairs, eager for the time to pass until seven-thirty. Half-way up she paused, half inclined to phone Carlo so that she could find out that much sooner. Only then did it occur to her that he could simply have left a message for her to phone him back, but he was coming round personally. Her heart froze; did that mean that his news was bad, that he didn't want to give her a shock over the phone?

By seven-thirty Petra had convinced herself that the worst had happened. She had got ready much too early, putting on a simple pink sleeveless shirtwaister that was the best of the few dresses she'd brought with her, her chestnut hair glowing on her shoulders, and wearing the minimum of make-up now that her face had started to tan. But that had only taken her a short time and by seven she hadn't been able to stand sitting in her room any longer and had come down to sit at one of the tables outside the café and wait.

At that time in the evening the streets were very crowded with people going out to eat. Even at Emilio's little café the tables were full and she had to share with an Austrian couple and their child. Vasco brought her a drink but she hardly touched it, her eyes probing the crowds in the direction that Carlo would come from the Palazzo, something telling her that she would know instinctively if the news was good or bad the moment she saw him.

She noticed him as soon as he came in sight because

he was that much taller than nearly everyone else. He was wearing a black evening suit that elegantly fitted his broad shoulders and athletic waist. Petra had her eyes glued on his face, her feelings a chaotic mixture of hope and dread, but she had been wrong, she could read nothing from his face. As he came nearer, she half rose, the suspense unbearable. Coming over to her table he took her limp hand and shook it. 'Good evening.'

'Well?' she burst out, unable to wait any longer. 'What is it? Have you found her?'

Carlo's eyes flickered over her anxious face and then he drew her down into her chair, sitting down beside her, the Austrians long since gone. 'No,' he answered steadily, which was at once relief and disappointment. 'But I have both a little good news and a little bad news for you.'

'Good news?' she exclaimed eagerly. 'What is it?'

He smiled. 'Only optimists ask for the good news first. We have found someone who thinks he may have seen Sara. But he isn't completely sure.'

'You have? Oh, how marvellous. Where? When? Who is he? I must go and see him and talk to him.' She was already half on her feet until Carlo put a restraining hand on her arm.

'Please, don't get so excited. The man is a ticket seller at the station. He thinks he sold a ticket to Paris to Sara, but he isn't certain and he can't remember when. I went to see him myself but he pointed out that the station is always so crowded that he often doesn't even have time to look at the people buying tickets, but he sometimes notices if a young girl buys one.'

Which was so typically male that Petra accepted it at once. 'But he couldn't remember when this was? Or whether Sara was alone?'

'No. But in the hope that he was right, I had my men

intensify their enquiries at the station and question all the staff, but there again we ran into a problem, because quite a few of the people who were working there when Sara was supposed to be in Venice have now gone on holiday themselves and we can only wait until they return before we can question them.'

'Yes, I see. But at least if someone thinks he saw her it means that Sara could have been here.'

'Yes,' Carlo agreed, but didn't look any too happy about it.

Petra followed the thought through and sighed. 'And it also means that she was okay when she left Venice so that whatever happened to her must have been on the way to or in Paris. And we're all wasting our time looking for her here.'

'That I'm afraid is the bad news,' Carlo agreed. 'And there is one other thing; I questioned Maria as you asked me to, but she left the Palazzo shortly after I left for America and went straight to her sister's, as I told you. She didn't come back until the day before my return. She said that she didn't see anyone.'

'So that's a dead end too?' Petra said hollowly.

'For the moment, yes. But we might be able to learn something more when the other station staff return from their holidays in a week or so.'

'And is that it? Is that all you've got to tell me?'

'Why, yes.'

She was suddenly, inexplicably angry. 'Couldn't you have told me that over the phone? Don't you realise what I've been going through while I've been sitting here waiting for you? I thought you had something so terrible to say that you couldn't tell me over the phone. Why else would you want to see me in person? I really thought ... And not only that I had to break a perfectly good date to meet you,' she finished, knowing

even as she said it that it was silly and he wouldn't care
anyway.

But his hand came out and covered hers. 'I'm sorry,'
he said sincerely. 'I didn't mean to frighten you. I
should have realised. I've noticed before how much this
worries you. And it didn't occur to me that you might
have a date. I didn't think you knew anyone in Venice.
Unless,' he let go of her hand and sat back, 'it was your
compatriot from the Consulate. Ah, I see it was.' His
dark eyes rested on her face for a moment and Petra
began to feel stupidly nervous again. 'But I was rather
hoping that you would have dinner with me and let me
show you something of Venice—my Venice. That's why
I came myself.'

Petra stared at him, taken completely by surprise.
'Oh, but I . . . I couldn't go out with you.'

'Why not?'

'Well, I don't . . . I mean I don't really know you.'

'You don't *really* know Signor Reid and yet you
consented to go out with him,' Carlo pointed out
mildly.

'But that's different.'

'Is it? Tell me why.' His eyes challenged her, amused
mockery in their depths.

'Don't laugh at me!' Petra exclaimed, suddenly tense.
'I don't know what it is about me that you always find
so damn funny, but I suppose you think it might be
amusing to take me out?'

Carlo leaned forward and shot out a hand to grab
her arm as she began to get to her feet. 'Sit down. Sit
down!' he repeated tersely as she pulled against him.
Realising that the people around were watching them,
Petra reluctantly obeyed, her chin set defiantly. 'I don't
find you funny,' Carlo told her firmly. 'If it appears so,
then I'm sorry. I know that you're worried and

unhappy and I merely wished to give you some amusement ...' he made a droll face. 'Oh, dear, unfortunate word. Some distraction, shall we say, which might help you to forget for tonight at least. Please, believe me.' And he smiled cajolingly.

The smile was really something, almost irresistible, but Petra didn't feel like forgiving him. She remembered Tony, beavering away in his office, waiting for her call. 'You really don't have to be kind ...' she began stiffly.

'Obviously not,' Carlo interrupted. 'I take it Signor Reid wasn't being kind, then?'

'I didn't mean ...' Petra broke off in some confusion, to realise she was being teased again. 'Look, for whatever reason, you don't have to take me out. I appreciate all the help you're giving me, I do really, but I'm quite okay on my own, you know. Okay, I'm worried about Sara, but just because I'm worried doesn't mean you have to worry, about me that is. I expect this is all a great nuisance to you really, and you're being awfully good about it, especially after the way I accused you at the beginning, and I can't ...'

Carlo reached a long finger across and placed it firmly on her lips, silencing her. Petra's eyes widened as she stared at him. 'I *want* to have dinner with you. Now, is it yes or no?'

Slowly he removed his finger and Petra immediately opened her mouth to refuse again, firmly this time, but then stopped. She gave a reluctant smile at his stern expression, and to her surprise heard herself say inexplicably, 'Yes,' instead of no, and was filled with a sudden surge of excitement and light-heartedness.

CHAPTER SIX

'Good,' Carlo said solemnly. 'I promise you you won't regret it.' He looked at her appealingly. 'Would it be possible for me to smile at you occasionally without you accusing me of making fun of you?'

Petra grinned. 'Sorry. I did rather fly off the handle, didn't I? I don't often lose my temper,' she confided, 'but I was a bit on edge.'

'And I pushed you over it. I deserve to be whipped.'

'*Now* you're treating me like a child,' she pointed out.

His eyes settled on her face, then flicked down. 'You're wrong. I would never treat you like a child,' he answered softly.

Petra's heart gave a peculiar kind of lurch. Wow! He really knew how to charm. But then, weren't all Latins supposed to be fantastic lovers? Perhaps he was like that with all women and it just came automatically. For a moment she was consumed with curiosity but then pushed the thought firmly out of her mind. She was merely being taken out to dinner by a chance acquaintance and that was all there was to it. 'Where are we going?' she asked brightly.

Carlo gave a small smile but successfully hid any amusement he might have felt at her swift change of subject. Getting to his feet, he pulled her chair back for her. 'I thought we might go to the Cipriani, it's on an island called La Giudecca to the south of the main city.'

She had heard of the Cipriani; who hadn't? It was one of the best and most expensive hotels in Venice, much favoured by passengers from the Orient Express,

116

and it also had an international reputation for the excellence of its cuisine. She immediately sat right down again.

His eyebrows lifted in surprise as Carlo said, 'Is anything the matter?'

'I don't want to go there,' Petra answered positively.

'But the food is very good.'

'Yes, I know, I've heard of it. But I'd rather not go there, thanks.'

'Well, all right. How about the Danieli, then?'

Oh Lord, that was the second priciest place in Venice! Again Petra shook her head. Carlo sat down again and put an elbow on the table, resting his chin on his hand as he looked at her rather exasperatedly. 'Tell me, just what have you got against those places? I've never known anyone refuse an offer to go to either of them before.'

'I haven't got anything against them; I'm sure they're marvellous.'

'But,' he prompted.

'Well . . .' Petra glanced down at her simple dress. 'I'm just not dressed for that kind of place.'

'Ah, I see.' Carlo nodded in understanding. 'And you couldn't . . .?'

'No,' she said firmly. 'I couldn't. This is the only half-way decent dress I have with me. And it's not even an evening dress. I'd feel really out of place at either the Cipriani or the Danieli.'

'You're wrong,' Carlo disagreed firmly. 'No one would care how you were dressed. But I understand. So—where do you think you would feel right and happy?'

Petra shrugged helplessly; she couldn't think of anywhere that she would like where Carlo, in his immaculate evening suit, wouldn't himself feel out of place. As it was, everyone who went by turned to look at the arrogantly handsome and obviously rich man sitting outside such a cheap little café, although it didn't seem to bother him at all. She gave a small laugh and, because she couldn't think of anything else, said facetiously, 'Here seems about the only place.'

'Here?' Carlo's eyebrows rose incredulously as he glanced inside the shabby little café. But then a devil-may-care look came into his eyes and he shrugged, saying flippantly, 'Why not?' and beckoned Emilio over.

Petra had never imagined that he would take her up on it and she half opened her mouth to stop him as he spoke in rapid Italian to Emilio, which caused the proprietor's eyes to nearly pop out in surprise. Emilio replied, gesturing eloquently to Carlo's dinner suit and then to the bare-topped tables, but Carlo's answer was swift and decisive.

He turned to Petra: 'They're getting a table inside ready for us. Let's have a drink while we wait, shall we?'

Vasco appeared with the drinks almost immediately, and Carlo lifted his glass to her, saying, 'Bon appetit,' rather wryly.

Petra didn't answer, merely nodded and sipped her drink; it was a red vermouth mixed with something else, soda water or lemonade probably, and tasted good in her dry throat. She was disappointed now that she'd ever mentioned the café; she would rather have gone almost anywhere with him than sit at one of the rickety tables inside the dingy place.

'What do you think of Venice now that you've seen more of it?' Carlo asked casually.

'Do you want the usual tourist phrases or what I really think?'

He gave her a quick glance, one eyebrow slightly raised. 'What you really think, of course.'

'Very well. I think Venice is like an old woman who was once beautiful but won't give in to age. Who covers herself with make-up so that from a distance she looks young, but when you get close you can see that it's only a façade and that there are irreparable cracks beneath the surface.'

Carlo looked at her with undisguised interest. 'That's a good simile, and mostly true, I'm afraid. I'm sorry you don't like Venice. Most people fall in love with the place and come back as often as they can.'

'I didn't say I didn't like it,' Petra pointed out. 'I think it's a wonderful city, but I'm not blind to its faults, that's all. But then, maybe the circumstances in which I'm seeing it aren't very propitious,' Petra told him with a hint of sadness.

'Obviously not. Maybe you'll look on it more favourably once you've found Sara.'

'If I ever find her.'

'Oh, I'm quite certain that if she's to be found, you'll find her.' He smiled at her. 'You're a very tenacious young lady. I know of no one else who would have hidden aboard a boat or tried to break into a house.'

'I didn't exactly try to break in.'

'Near enough.' He tapped her on the nose in mock sternness, then glanced towards the door, drained his glass and stood up. 'I think they're ready for us now. Shall we go in?'

Petra looked round and saw Vasco standing at the door of the café, holding it open for them. And she saw, too, that as the customers around them had left, their chairs had been propped against the tables as if the place was closed. She had been so absorbed in talking to Carlo that she hadn't even noticed before.

'Why has he done that?'

'I told the patron to close the café.'

'You mean you just took over the place?' Petra stared at him incredulously.

Carlo shrugged. 'If we're going to eat here we may as well do so in comfort.'

Unable to find words to describe her feelings, Petra walked into the café and found that the inside had been transformed. Nearly all the tables had been taken out and there was just one in the middle of the room. It was covered with a white damask cloth and set with gleaming silver cutlery and fragile glass; there was even a bowl of fresh flowers in the centre. The lights were dimmed, hiding the plastic shabbiness, and from somewhere Emilio had magicked some tall pot plants as an extra screen. There was even music playing softly in the background.

Petra blinked and blinked again when Emilio, in a spotlessly clean shirt and black suit that smelt of mothballs, bowed her to her seat. Then with a flourish he presented her with a flower for her dress. Carlo sat down opposite, not attempting to hide his amusement at her expression.

'Perhaps you'd like me to pin your flower on for you?' he offered.

She thought of his hands touching her skin and said hastily, 'I think I can manage, thanks.' She was overawed at the transformation and asked, 'How did you manage all this? And without any warning?'

'Oh, it's amazing what people can do when given a challenge and the price is right,' he added with a grin.

'But the cloth and the silver—it's beautiful. Did you have it sent round from your palazzo?'

'No. I expect the patron had it packed away in a cupboard somewhere, to be brought out only on special occasions. Most Italian families have, and they hand the things down from one generation to the next.' He turned away as Emilio came up with some wine and they went through the ceremony of trying it. 'Tonight we're going to have a traditionally Venetian meal,' he informed her as Vasco brought up the first course. Adding rather sardonically, 'Perhaps you will like our food as much as our time-raddled city.'

He was right; Petra did like the food. They started with something he called *prosciutto crudo*, which turned out to be raw ham with delicious fresh figs, served skinned and ice-cold. This was followed by fish soup and then by the biggest scampi that Petra had ever seen; six of them overflowed her plate. By then she was nearly full but Emilio insisted they try his *fegato alla Veneziana*, which sounded terribly grand but turned out to be fried liver and onions, one of the few traditional Venetian dishes, but so beautifully cooked that it was irresistible. They finished with ice-cream as only the Italians know how to make it, and then large cups of espresso coffee.

'Mmm, that was delicious.' Petra sat back, feeling as if her stomach had doubled in size. Gradually during the meal, she had lost her first nervousness and tension, had listened when Carlo told her what the authorities were trying to do to save Venice and the massive job they had before them. He told her about the Venice in Peril Fund and the work it was carrying out, and described how, in the last fifty years, pollution had done more harm to Venice than all the last five hundred years put together.

As Carlo talked, he showed her a side of himself that she hadn't seen before; it was obvious that he cared a great deal about the city and that he was personally involved, devoting a great deal of his time to trying to save it. It was a facet of his character that Petra hadn't seen before, but then she really didn't know him at all. Gradually she was drawn under the spell of his smile, was relaxed by his charm and wooed by his dominant, almost mesmerising masculinity. She found herself animatedly discussing a variety of topics that led naturally from one to another, from art to fox-hunting, on which she had very definite views. And she laughed a lot, too, because Carlo had a dry wit that matched her own sense of humour, and she completely forgot all her worries and cares.

It grew hot in the little café and Petra drank the last of her wine. Emilio and Vasco had disappeared into the kitchens and they were alone in the circle of light. Carlo had a balloon of brandy in his right hand that he moved in small circles, watching the liquid catch the light as it swirled in the crystal glass. He was completely relaxed, his head slightly tilted so that his features were thrown into sharp outlines, his mouth smiling slightly as he listened to her. Petra was telling him how her parents had been sent to live in the West Indies but as she looked at Carlo, her voice slowly died in her throat, all else forgotten as she gazed at him.

His eyes came quickly up to meet hers and his hand grew still. Petra tried to look away, but Carlo's dark eyes held her prisoner and reality faded away. Slowly he set down his glass and reached out to cover her hand where it lay on the table. It fluttered wildly for a moment, but then grew still and Carlo tightened his grip. His eyes never leaving hers, he stood up and drew her to her feet, then pulled her gently into his arms, holding her close against him as he began to slowly move in time to the music that played softly in the background. Petra danced as though hypnotised, intensely aware of his nearness and the hardness of his

lean body whenever they touched. Her own pulses were
racing crazily, and she couldn't even begin to think
why. Dancing with Carlo was somehow different from
dancing with anyone else. Perhaps it was the fairy-tale
atmosphere, the way a few words from him had made
the little café into a magic place for themselves alone.
Petra had the feeling that when the clock struck twelve
it would become dark and dingy again, so she let herself
fall under the spell, held in the strong circle of his arms,
as they moved slowly round the floor. She gave a long
sigh of pure pleasure and Carlo drew her closer, holding
her hand against his chest. Slowly she raised her eyes to
look at him and found him gazing down at her with a
strange, almost surprised look in his dark eyes. He
stood still, his eyes fixed on her face for a long moment,
then he said softly in an odd voice, 'Petra.'

'Yes.'

His hand tightened for a second, but then he gave a
small shrug as if remembering where he was and said,
again in that odd, unsure tone, 'Let's go for a walk?'

Without waiting for her to agree, he opened the door
of the café and they walked out together into the night.

A brilliant moon filled the sky so that there was
almost no need for the light from the ornate lamp-posts
in the middle of the narrow street. Carlo took her arm
and put it through his so they walked close together.
There were many other people about, strolling along,
but Petra was hardly aware of them, alive only to
Carlo, to the disturbing sensations that his nearness
gave her, and to the magic quality of the night. They
didn't seem to be heading in any particular direction,
but presently they crossed a little canal in front of an
ornate church and came out into the long colonnaded
rectangle of St Mark's Square. On their left a small
orchestra was playing outside one of the cafés and they

went to sit at one of the tables and drink more coffee as they listened.

They sat quite close, so that sometimes their arms or knees would touch, and when Carlo had finished his coffee, he casually put his hand over hers, idly playing with her fingers. Petra stiffened for a moment and then relaxed, knowing it didn't mean anything; but it was the sexiest sensation, sending odd shivers down her spine. She stood it for as long as she could, but then her fingers suddenly tightened. Carlo looked at her, then deliberately raised her hand to his mouth and kissed each of her fingers in turn, his eyes fixed steadily on her face.

He's flirting with me! Petra realised in astonishment as she gazed back at him with a slightly dazed expression in her hazel eyes. She tried to pull herself together, but it was impossible when he was looking at her like that. And besides, there had been too much wine and candlelight, too much music and moonlight, and there was too much magic in the air.

Petra felt as if she was floating about a foot in the air as they left the café and walked through the Piazzetta down to the canal. Across St Mark's Basin they could see the floodlit Palladian church of Saint Giorgio Maggiore standing on its own island across the water and beside it another campanile similar to the one in St Mark's Square, and just across the canal was another church, the one everyone called Saint Salute. Venice was full of churches, all of them beautiful in one way or another. They stood for a while looking out at the lights reflected in the moonlit water, then Carlo turned her to face him. 'Will you come for a gondola ride with me?'

'Oh, I'd love to. I haven't been in one yet,' Petra exclaimed with real delight.

'Then it will be my pleasure to take you. This way.'

He led her down to the canal, but to Petra's surprise
didn't approach any of the gondoliers who were waiting
to be hired, but lifted his arm in a signal to a boat
moored some way from the others. It came at once, the
gondolier wearing the traditional jacket and straw hat,
and manoeuvring expertly to draw alongside them. The
gondola, too, was in the traditional glossy black but the
paintwork shone with care and attention and the bright
silver of the fittings glistened in the lamplight. There
was also a crest painted on the side that Petra had seen
before on Carlo's crested notepaper. My God, he even
owned his own gondola!

For a moment she was too overawed to move, but
then Carlo helped her in and put his arm round her as
they lay back against the cushions. The gondolier poled
out into the canal and set off through the city.
Somewhere ahead of them was a serenade boat with a
singer and an accordionist on board, the sound carrying
back to them over the water. Everyone seemed to be on
the water tonight; there were lots of other gondolas as
well as the vaporettos, it was like being on a busy road,
but presently Carlo said something to the gondolier and
he turned off the main canal into a much smaller one
where there were more ornate lamps and low bridges
that cast dark patches of shadow across the water. On
either side there were houses with windows set low near
the canal with black wrought-iron balconies heavy with
pots of geraniums and flowers that scented the night
air. They passed a little restaurant where diners lingered
over their meal under a trellis of purple bougainvillaea,
then the oasis of light was gone as they slid under
another bridge into darkness again.

Petra turned to Carlo to try to thank him, to tell him
that the ride would stay in her memory for ever, but
somehow, when she looked at him, the words died in

her throat and she felt too choked up to speak. He lifted a hand to gently push a stray lock of hair back from her face and she suddenly thought that he was going to kiss her. And with the thought came the heady certainty that she *wanted* him to kiss her. She wanted to know what it would be like when those hard, experienced lips met hers. No, took hers; for somehow she knew that Carlo was the kind of lover whose women would give him anything he wanted.

His hand rested on her neck for a moment and she held her breath, but then he gave a small smile and sat back, pointing out a house where Byron had once stayed. Two minutes later they had left the small waterway and entered the brightness of the Grand Canal again. Petra felt an idiotic wish to turn right round and go back. She felt light-headed and there seemed to be far more stars in the sky then there had been before.

They went under the Rialto Bridge which was lined with people looking at the traffic on the canal, past the rich palazzos which were mostly museums and hotels now, and Petra recognised Carlo's own house. For a breathless moment she wondered if he intended to take her there and her body tensed, but the gondolier poled past and she slowly relaxed.

Twenty minutes later they were back at St Mark's and the gondolier helped her out. It was quieter now with a lot less people around; the orchestra had gone home and the shutters were pulled down over the arched windows of the shops and cafés in the square. Carlo took her hand and they strolled in silence through the quiet, moonlit city. They walked slowly, passing from squares to narrow alleys between high walls, along cobbled ways and over hump-backed bridges, the moon often lost behind the tall buildings so that the only light was from the street lights, too ornate to give more than a small glow at irregular intervals.

Emerging from an alleyway, they found a small canal cutting across their path, its still surface mirrored in the moonlight so that it looked like a glistening silver ribbon. At the top of the bridge that crossed it, they tacitly paused for a moment and Petra gave a long sigh of delight as she took in each detail of the scene, trying to hold it indelibly in her memory.

'So now,' Carlo said softly, 'what do you think of Venice?'

'It's a night city. I hadn't realised that before. In the moonlight it's beautiful.'

'Like an old woman who looks young again in the candlelight,' Carlo teased. 'And will you come back again?'

'Perhaps,' Petra answered, her shoulders drooping as she suddenly remembered Sara.

Carlo put a long finger under her chin, making her look at him. 'Not tonight,' he said gently. 'Promise me that tonight you will think only of Venice.'

Her eyes went to his mouth and she wondered again what it would be like if he kissed her. 'All right,' she answered in little more than a whisper.

'Good girl.' He straightened up. 'Now, I have another part of Venice to show you.' Taking her arm firmly in his he began to walk her briskly along as somewhere a clock chimed three, its hollow notes echoing through the quiet city.

He took her back to his palazzo but led her straight through it to his boat moored by the steps, and then the powerful vessel was free of its ropes and surging up the centre of the Canal, its wake a turbulent fluorescence in the moonlight. Petra stood beside Carlo, gripping the handrail, enjoying the breeze that blew her hair around

her head and cooled her hot skin, enjoying their speed
as the palaces of the ancient city flashed past. Turning
to him, she gave a laugh of pure exhilaration and he
laughed with her, putting his arm round her waist and
drawing her close beside him. They flashed under the
Academy bridge and out into St Mark's Basin, then
they were out into the lagoon that surrounded Venice
where the waves caught them and spray splashed
against the sides. For a while they sped along parallel to
the Lido, its white deserted beaches ghostly in the
moonlight, but then they were past and Carlo was
picking his way surely through the maze of islands that
surrounded the actual city of Venice and out into the
open lagoon. Turning down the throttle, the boat came
almost to a halt, the engine just ticking over enough to
hold the boat in position.

Petra looked round into a sea of darkness with only
the faint lights from the islands in the distance. 'Where are
we?' she asked in puzzlement. 'Why have we come here?'

'You'll see, shortly.' Carlo glanced at his watch in the
green light of the dashboard. 'Not long to wait now.'

Petra looked again into the darkness and shivered
suddenly, thinking of the water all around them.
Slipping off his jacket, Carlo put it round her shoulders.
'Sorry, I should have realised you were cold.' And he
drew her down beside him on an upholstered seat that
ran along the side of the cockpit.

She wasn't really cold, but Petra didn't refuse the
jacket. It was still warm from his body and when she
turned her head she could smell faint traces of his
aftershave on the collar. Taking out a cigarette, Carlo
lit it and leaned back, his arm negligently across her
shoulders. She sneaked a look at his profile and saw
that the green glow from the dashboard had hardened
his features, giving an almost satanic look of cruelty to

his face. But then he turned towards her and the cruelty was gone, leaving sensitivity in its place, especially around his mouth.

Kiss me, please kiss me. The wish was so strong that for a moment Petra thought that she'd spoken the words aloud, and felt an overwhelming sense of relief when she realised she hadn't. But had he guessed her thoughts? Her eyes searched his face anxiously in the darkness, but he turned away and after a moment said softly, 'Look.'

Following his gaze, Petra couldn't for a moment see anything at all, but then realised that the sky was beginning to lighten in the east. Blackness gave way to dull grey and then the first golden red shafts of sun promised the dawn of a beautiful day. The sky began to glow with colour: red, orange, purple and flame; setting the horizon on fire and taking her breath away as Petra gazed spellbound, enthralled by the sight. The rays of morning ran across the lagoon and caught Venice in their grasp, turning the buildings into gold that quickly spread until the whole city was ablaze under the aubade of dawn.

Only when the sun came up completely above the horizon did Petra let out a long, long sigh of pure enchantment and turn to Carlo. There were tears on her cheeks as she said simply, 'Thank you. Oh, *thank you* for that.'

Lifting a hand, he gently wiped away the tears, his eyes on her face, and then he slowly bent to kiss her.

His lips were hard, as she had guessed they would be, but he was gentle for all that, his mouth exploring hers and seeking rather than demanding a response, which she willingly gave. Strange disturbing sensations began to wake in her and she felt a deep hunger that she'd never experienced before. But all too soon he drew back and smiled down at her. 'Good morning,' he said lazily.

Petra's chest was so tight she could hardly speak. She gazed at him wide-eyed, lips still parted from his kiss and wishing fervently that he had gone on kissing her for just a little longer. Or a whole lot longer. The thought made her gulp and somehow pull herself together. 'G-good morning,' she managed, with a desperate attempt at a casual smile. 'Is—is it always as overwhelming as that?'

He looked amused. 'I suppose you *do* mean the dawn?'

'What? Oh!' Petra coloured. 'Yes, of course.'

Carlo laughed and started the engine, but this time sailed more sedately, pausing on the way at the Porto di Lido to show her the passageway from Venice out into the open Adriatic where the Doges used to go every year to wed the sea, throwing a golden ring into it as a token of their perpetual rule.

'What happened?' Petra asked. 'Did the ceremony die out?'

'Napoleon happened,' Carlo answered with a short laugh. 'But they perform the ceremony every year again now—for the tourists.'

He had sounded a little bitter, but Petra said warmly, 'Good, I'm glad they still do it, even if they don't really believe in it any more. At least it's something active that's being preserved, not just another building.'

There was a rather closed expression on his face and for a moment Petra thought that she'd offended him; after all it was his city and nothing to do with her how they ran it, but then Carlo smiled. 'You're right, of course. Anything that can be preserved, in whatever form, is well worth the keeping.'

He opened the throttle and the boat purred along, past the offshore islands, hazy now in the early morning mists, and into the wide basin of water that ran alongside the dozens of little islands, sewn together by innumerable bridges, that made up Venice proper.

She had expected Carlo to take the boat to his palazzo again, but instead he went a little further on and tied up at the vaporetto jetty nearest to the café. It was still very early with hardly anyone about as he helped her ashore and they walked slowly through alleyways inhabited only by tiger-striped cats, plump from their night of foraging. The clear light of morning gave a new dimension to the city that Petra found hard to explain; it was as if it was no longer old but had just been built and people would soon come out of their houses in the traditional dress and tricorn hats of three centuries ago. As if Venice had been caught up under a Sleeping Beauty enchantment and had lain asleep for hundreds of years.

Petra didn't speak for fear of breaking the spell, and Carlo, too, seemed content to walk along in silence, his arm lightly around her waist under his jacket. They came to the back entrance of the café all too quickly and Petra turned to thank him and gave him back his coat. Her heart beating, she wondered whether he would kiss her again and had a fierce wish that he would, but then realised that the dawn out there on the open sea had been the right moment, not here in the grotty courtyard. So she firmly held out her hand to him and said sincerely, 'Thank you for a marvellous evening. For the gondola ride. And I can't begin to describe how wonderful it was to see the dawn. I shall never forget it, not for as long as I live.'

'Or me?' he asked lightly, taking her hand.

'Or you,' she agreed after a moment, her voice not quite steady.

He nodded, then bent to kiss her hand, the gesture supremely elegant in these shabby surroundings, then walked away, pausing at the corner to turn and wave goodbye.

CHAPTER SEVEN

PETRA let herself into the café and went as quietly as she could up the creaking staircase, but she needn't have bothered because just as she got to the second landing, Emilio's door opened and he came out, yawning and scratching himself. He looked at her in owlish surprise, but Petra quickly muttered, *'Buon giorno,'* and ran up the rest of the stairs to her room.

It was six o'clock and she should have been exhausted but strangely Petra didn't feel at all tired, even though she undressed and got into bed. Her mind, in fact, felt exhilarated, teeming with thoughts and memories that chased each other through her head, one hardly formulated before another pushed it aside. It had been such an unusual, memorable night, one that she would truly never forget, as she'd told Carlo. Her thoughts quietened, centring on him, on the way he'd looked out there in the half-light and the way he'd kissed her. For a few minutes she let herself drown in the memory of it, but then the sound of Vasco going down to the bathroom on the lower landing, whistling a pop tune as he went, brought her sharply back to reality. So she'd been kissed by a sexy Italian Count; it would be something to tell her grandchildren one day, but it was no big deal. Certainly nothing to get excited about, she told herself sternly. It hadn't meant anything. It was just that the time was right and he'd kissed her. Thinking back on it, she'd probably made it pretty plain that that was what she expected, Petra realised with sudden and fierce embarrassment. He had just been giving a treat to a poor little English girl that he probably felt sorry for, and had made her evening by giving her the kiss she so obviously wanted.

Petra's face burned and she turned it into the pillow, wondering just how big a fool she'd made of herself. But it hadn't seemed like that at the time so why should she think so now? Restlessly she sat up and looked around the little room, clearly lit by the growing sunlight seeping through the shutters. It was less than half a mile away from the palazzo but a world away in comparison. But her own home back in England was quite luxurious when compared to it, too.

Getting out of bed, Petra threw open the shutters, knowing that she wouldn't be able to sleep. Her eyes went automatically towards the rooftops near the Grand Canal. Had Carlo gone to bed to snatch what sleep he could, or was he, too, lying awake, thinking of the night that had gone? Would he think that it had been a pleasant evening, or was he congratulating himself on having given someone he felt sorry for a night to remember, something that she would never otherwise have experienced? Well, she'd certainly assured him of that. He must have thought her incredibly naive the way she'd gazed up at him and told him how wonderful it all was, Petra thought, furious with herself for letting him take pity on her.

She tried to shut out the unpleasant thoughts and recapture the magic of the evening, but it was impossible now, however hard she tried. Sighing, Petra began to dress, wondering why it had all suddenly gone sour, and feeling rather like Cinderella must have done when she got back from the ball and found the same old kitchen and piles of work waiting to be done. She smiled at herself at the incongruity of the thought and decided that maybe it was just as well; it wouldn't do to

get any ideas about Carlo. For all that he was willing to
flirt a little to make her evening, he wasn't about to let
himself even think of getting serious about some foreign
girl he'd met by chance and hardly knew. Not that she
wanted to get serious, of course. No way. Carlo was
just a playboy. It was men like Tony Reid that you
actually married.

At thought of Tony, Petra lifted a horrified hand to
her mouth. My God, she was supposed to have phoned
him last night, but she hadn't even given it a thought
after Carlo had asked her to have dinner with him. She
just wasn't the type of person to forget a promise and it
made her feel terribly guilty. Now she would have to try
and get hold of Tony and put it right. Oh darn! What
with embarrassment over one man and guilt over
another this was turning into one hell of a day. And it
had started off so beautifully, too. Gritting her teeth,
Petra picked up her bag and went down to the café to
have some breakfast.

Emilio greeted her with a wide grin, although his
wife gave her a disapproving look when she glanced
up from the cooker as Petra went through the
kitchen. Vasco, too, gave her an odd, rather leering
kind of smile as he said good morning. There was
something about the smile that Petra didn't like, but
it wasn't until she was half way through breakfast
that she suddenly realised that Emilio had seen her
come in at six o'clock in the morning and probably
thought that she had spent the night with Carlo!
Beckoning Vasco over, Petra said in careful English
so that he would be sure to understand, 'Will you
please thank Emilio for our meal here last night?
Count Berini took me for a ride in his gondola and
then to watch the sun rise in his boat. Do you
understand? We went for a ride in his boat.'

Vasco nodded, but again gave her that knowing smile. '*Si*. Is very comfortable in the cabin, no?'

'Oh, for heaven's sake!' Petra got up and walked out of the café, fuming. Just because Carlo had the reputation of being a womaniser they automatically thought that she had let him make love to her. Huh! Chance would be a fine thing! That thought made her choke and start to cough.

'Are you all right?'

Someone patted her on the back and she looked up, eyes watering, to find Tony beside her. 'Oh!' Cough. 'Hi, Tony, I was just going to find you.'

'And I was doing the same. Are you okay now?'

'Yes, thanks. Something went down the wrong way. Tony, I'm sorry about last night but . . .'

'What happened to you? I was worried. I phoned the café about eleven but they said you weren't there.'

'No, well, actually I wasn't,' Petra admitted uncomfortably.

'What was it? Did Berini bring you any news?' Tony asked sharply.

'Some. He said he found someone at the station who thinks he might have seen Sara.'

'Might have?'

'Yes, the man wasn't absolutely sure.'

'And was that all?'

'He also told me that he'd questioned his housekeeper, but she was away most of the time that he was and hadn't been back to the house, so she hadn't seen anyone that shouldn't be there.' Petra paused reflectively. 'I still can't understand why she seems to dislike and resent me, though.'

'And that was all Berini had to tell you?' And when Petra nodded. 'He could have told you all that in five minutes over the phone. Why did he see you himself?'

'Petra shrugged. 'I don't know.' But she didn't look at him.

'It couldn't have taken that long; why didn't you phone me afterwards? I was at the office until nearly ten.'

'He didn't go straightaway,' she admitted unhappily. 'We talked and then, as neither of us had eaten, we had a meal at the café.'

'At the café? Berini? I don't believe it. He wouldn't be seen dead in a place like that.'

The fact that Petra had thought exactly the same thing made her say perversely, 'I don't see why you say that; he was quite happy to eat there.'

Tony's mouth grew grim. 'I beg your pardon.'

'Oh, Tony please.' Petra caught his arm as he half turned away. 'Look, I'm really sorry about last night, but he was telling me about the Venice in Peril campaign, and then he more or less insisted that I have dinner with him, and after that it was too late to phone.'

She looked at him pleadingly and after a moment he smiled at her again. 'I'm sorry, too. I'm just jealous, I suppose. I was really looking forward to seeing you last night.'

'Can't we make it tonight, instead?'

'All right, that's a date. Let's hope Berini doesn't take it into his head to tell you to meet him again,' he added so wryly that Petra knew it still rankled. But he took her hand and said, 'Walk me to the office.'

As they strolled along they discussed the possible sighting of Sara at the station but Tony wasn't at all encouraging. 'It could have been anyone.'

'I know,' Petra sighed. 'I've thought I've seen her here in Venice several times myself. One poor fair-haired girl must think I'm utterly mad. I've grabbed her twice already.'

They parted at the door of the Consular building and then there was nothing for Petra to do but to wander aimlessly round the city again showing her photo of Sara, but now when people shook their heads, one or two of them mentioned that they had already been shown the photograph, so it was obvious that she was covering ground where either Carlo's men or the Consul's agents had already been, which made it seem more then ever like a waste of time. But that didn't matter so much because somehow the city looked different today, as if she was seeing it with new eyes. Instead of seeing it as a city sinking beneath hundreds of years of decay, she saw it as a place that was gradually being saved to last for another five hundred years. She saw what had been restored rather than the hundreds of things that still needed to be done, and it was only after quite some time that Petra realised she was looking at Venice through the eyes of a native, through Carlo's eyes in fact.

At lunchtime she made her way to the Academy bridge, intending to have a drink and a sandwich at one of the cafés skirting the Giudecca Canal, an area where she hadn't yet made any enquiries. As she reached the middle of the bridge, Petra paused, just as every tourist did, to look up the Grand Canal and watch the kaleidoscope of traffic weaving its intricate and hazardous pattern on the water. A vaporetto came under the bridge beneath her feet and Petra glanced idly down, then froze. There was a girl sitting near the front of the boat, her fair hair blown about her head by the breeze. A girl who looked exactly like Sara. She was half-turned away from Petra, looking up at a tall, good-looking young man, his fair hair cut very short. Petra's heart leapt and she turned to run across the bridge to try and catch the boat at the next vaporetto stop. But then she stopped, remembering how many other blonde girls she had gone chasing after, only to be bitterly disappointed. This time she would be sensible. Sara wasn't going to turn up safe and well in Venice; that would be too much of a miracle to hope for.

Petra spent the rest of the day in areas she hadn't been to before, showing her photo of Sara without success and feeling more and more that the whole thing was futile. If it wasn't that she was seeing the city now as a place of hope rather than despair, she would have felt pretty desperate herself. It was weeks now since Sara had disappeared, with no clue whatsoever except the dubious recognition by the man at the station. Sadly, Petra realised that she couldn't leave it any longer; Sara's parents would have to be traced and informed.

That afternoon Petra went back to the café earlier than she normally did; the hot sun and hard pavements were just too much, she felt sticky and grubby and longed for a bath. The café was still open, but it was that in between time; too late for mid-afternoon drinks, too early for a meal, and so there were few people outside and none in. It was Vasco's time off but Emilio sat behind the counter, reading the paper. He looked up when she came in and began to talk to her very fast, gesturing skywards with his hands. At the sound of his voice his wife, whose name Petra had never heard, came out of the kitchen to join him. She looked more disapproving then ever and Petra's heart sank. The only word she recognised in what Emilio was saying was '*camera*' which she knew meant room, and that, coupled with his upward gestures, made her afraid that they wanted her to leave the café. Oh darn! And all because she'd spent a completely innocent few hours with Carlo. It would be well nigh impossible to find somewhere else in Venice at this time of year, especially somewhere so cheap. Unless Tony knew of a cheap hotel.

She nodded dully and went slowly upstairs to her room, wondering whether she was supposed to leave at once or could stay for the night; surely they wouldn't just throw her out at a moment's notice? As she opened the door of her room she smelt the roses. There was a whole bunch of them, two dozen at least, perfect golden cream rosebuds that filled the room with their scent and reminded her vividly of England, of her garden at home early on a fine June morning when the dew still clung to the rose petals. Dropping her bag, Petra quickly crossed to the dressing-table on which the roses had been placed in a big vase and lowered her head to drink in their scent, gently stroking the petals of one of the flowers with her finger tip. They were beautiful, perfectly lovely.

There was a small, sealed envelope propped against the vase which she quickly opened. There were only two men in Venice who would send her flowers, but she knew, even before she read the card, that they were from Carlo. It said simply, 'In memory of a golden dawn.'

Impulsively Petra turned and ran down the stairs again to the phone, using it whether Emilio approved or not. A man answered but it wasn't Carlo. 'Er—could I speak to Count Berini, please?' And when the man asked who she was, 'Will you tell him it's Petra Thornton.'

She heard the man repeat her name and then Carlo was on the line. 'Hallo, Petra.'

'Thank you for the roses,' she said with warm gratitude. 'They're exquisite, beautiful.'

'I'm glad you like them.'

'Oh, I do. I've never had roses given to me before,'

she told him with simple artlessness. As soon as she said it, Petra wished she hadn't, thinking how childish it sounded.

But he didn't seem to notice. 'Think of me when you look at them,' he said lightly. 'And of last night.'

'Of course. I'm sure I didn't thank you properly this morning. I really had a wonderful time,' she assured him, forgetting how she'd told herself off only a few hours ago for being so enthusiastic.

'Perhaps we can do it again soon.'

'Oh, but I didn't mean . . .' Petra began in dismay.

'No, but I did,' Carlo said crisply. 'Can I phone you tomorrow?'

'I—I'm afraid I won't be here tomorrow.'

'You're going back to England?' he asked in sharp surprise.

'No. At least, not unless I have to. But I've got to leave the café and I don't know where I'll be staying yet.'

'Why have you got to leave?'

That was the last thing Petra wanted to explain. 'It really doesn't matter. I'll let you know when I find somewhere else.'

'I'm sorry if I sound offensive, Petra, but have you run out of money?'

'Oh no, it's nothing like that, really.'

'Then why?' She hesitated and he added, 'Please tell me.'

'I'd really rather not. It doesn't matter, honestly.'

'If you don't tell me,' he said grimly, 'I shall come round there and find out.'

Petra groaned inwardly, then said reluctantly, 'Oh, all right. They want me to leave because I was out all night with you. I've tried to tell Vasco that we were out on your boat, but they don't seem to believe me.

Or that's what I think it is; the language thing doesn't help.'

'Let me speak to Emilio,' Carlo ordered. 'And please don't argue,' he added as she opened her mouth to do just that. 'Just put him on the line.'

Petra recognised the note of authority when she heard it and called Emilio over, standing to one side and smiling embarrassedly at his wife while he talked.

The two men spoke for some time with a lot of gesturing on Emilio's part, then he gave the receiver back to her.

'I'm afraid it's Emilio's wife who disapproves of you,' Carlo told her, sinking her hopes. 'But don't bother to try to find a hotel. I've told Emilio that you will be staying here and . . .'

'What?' Petra exclaimed. 'D-did you mean at the Palazzo?'

'Yes. If you pack your case Emilio will carry it round for you.'

'But—but I couldn't. That is—I mean, thank you very much but I couldn't possibly come and stay with you.'

'But it's entirely my fault that you can no longer stay at the café,' Carlo pointed out with a logic that Petra hadn't even thought of. 'I should have realised how it would look, keeping you out that late.'

'But that's ridiculous! Oh, sorry. I didn't mean that the way it sounded. But of course it isn't your fault. I'll just find another hotel and . . .'

'If you're thinking of your reputation,' Carlo interrupted mildly, 'may I remind you that Maria is here and lives in the house.'

'I wasn't.' Petra's cheeks flamed. 'It's just that you don't have to do this.'

'But I want to. This whole thing started with

someone using my name and I feel very involved. And I'm sure we could work towards finding Sara much better if you were living here.' Petra quite failed to see the logic in that but evidently Carlo could. He went on firmly, 'So pack your things and let Emilio bring you round. I'd come myself but I have a business associate with me at the moment. Maria will be expecting you,' he added.

She stood silently, not knowing what to say, what to do, but Carlo seemed to take her acceptance for granted because he said, 'See you later,' and then put down the phone.

She packed in a kind of daze and paid Emilio the rent she owed him before saying goodbye to his wife and walking with him through the streets, her roses clutched in her hand, her hold-all over her arm, while Emilio puffed along with her case. Obviously Emilio didn't disapprove of her because he kept giving her big grins, but Petra tried not to look him in the face too much in case she blushed at what he was thinking of her going to stay with Carlo, housekeeper or no. At the palazzo Maria opened the door to them, looking as disapproving as Emilio's wife had, but she had obviously been given her orders because she stepped back to let Petra in and then took her up to a bright and airy room on the second floor that looked out over the canal. The housekeeper went to open the case to unpack for her, but Petra hastily said she'd do it herself, which only made Maria frown even more. But Petra didn't care: she still felt in a kind of excited daze and hurried to push open the shutters as soon as the woman had gone. For a long time she just leaned over the window sill, drinking her fill of the wonderful view over the city and to the islands beyond, then turned to really look at the

room Carlo had given her. Compared to her old
room at the café it was palatial, although in fact it
wasn't terribly large. Its most attractive feature was a
four-poster bed, but a light, delicate one hung with
white lace, not one of the great monsters hung with
heavy curtains that you saw in museums. The walls of
the room were covered with pale blue silk and the
furniture, too, was light with a mixture of modern
comfort and antique elegance. Opening off the room
was a mirror-lined bathroom equipped with thick
towels with Carlo's monogram on them.

Petra first arranged her roses in a vase and then
unpacked slowly, enjoying the thick carpet under her
bare feet and the opulence of the room after the
shabbiness of the café. From the ridiculous to the
sublime, she thought, luxuriating in a bath overflowing
with bubbles, and wished heartily that she had the
clothes with her she had left behind in Paris as she
dressed to go downstairs.

Carlo didn't seem to be about. The room he used to
work in was empty when she glanced inside and he
wasn't in any of the other reception rooms. After a few
moments' hesitation Petra picked up the phone in
Carlo's study and dialled the Consulate, sure that Carlo
wouldn't mind. Tony had already left but she reached
him at his private number. It was only when she began
to tell him where she was that she realised just how
hard it was going to be to explain.

'You're staying where?' Tony said incredulously.

Again Petra explained about Emilio's wife, but in
doing so she also had to admit that she'd been out all
night with Carlo.

'You didn't mention that before,' Tony pointed out
stiffly.

'Didn't I? Probably because it wasn't important.'

He didn't make any comment about that, but said, 'And what about our date tonight? Is it on or not?'

'Of course it's on,' Petra answered after a moment's frantic hesitation as she wondered whether Carlo would mind. 'But I'll meet you somewhere else if you'd rather.'

'No, I'll call for you at the palazzo. See you in about an hour.'

'Yes, okay. 'Bye Tony.' She put the phone down and turned to see that Carlo was standing in the doorway.

He had a stern look on his face that turned to rather a stiff smile of greeting. 'Hallo. I'm sorry I wasn't able to welcome you myself, but I trust that Maria did everything that was necessary?'

'Yes, she did. Thank you.' Now that she was there, Petra felt completely tongue-tied, which was unusual for her; she usually talked too much when she was nervous.

Carlo came into the room and shut the door. He was dressed more casually than she'd ever seen him before, in dark trousers and matching shirt, open at the neck and with the cuffs turned back. 'I trust you found your room comfortable?'

'Oh yes, it's a lovely room.' Petra looked at him uncertainly, he seemed so distant somehow, and she wondered whether he was regretting having asked her or whether he had merely done so out of a sense of obligation. 'I hope you don't mind me using the phone? I'll pay for the call of course,' she added stiffly.

He looked directly at her then. 'Don't be silly. I couldn't help overhearing; I take it that you're going out with Reid tonight?'

'Yes. It's all right, isn't it? I was supposed to go out with him last night but . . .'

'But you had to break it off because of me. Yes, of

course it's all right,' he said rather impatiently. 'You must do exactly as you wish. You must treat the palazzo as if it were your home.' He turned abruptly. 'Let's go down to the library, shall we?'

Treat it as if it were my home! Petra laughed to herself at the impossibility of the idea as she followed Carlo down the stairs. It might be home to him but to anyone else it was like living in a beautiful and luxurious museum.

She liked the library, it smelt of leather and books, and it wasn't so large as some of the other reception rooms. There were shelves of books from floor to ceiling on two of the walls, but the others were crammed with pictures, not only paintings but framed photographs as well, some of them quite recent. While Carlo poured her a drink Petra went to look at the more modern ones and found that they were of Carlo at his old school, mixed up among the rugger team in shorts and jersey, or the cricket team in whites. And there he was at university in a dark blue shirt and holding an oar beside a long rowing boat.

'Did you row for Oxford?' Petra asked in surprise, her eyes widening.

Carlo came over and handed her a drink, looking at the photograph with her. 'Yes. It seems a lifetime ago now.'

Petra gazed at him with new respect. 'My brother's up at Oxford. He wants to get into the university boat team but he said that you have to be almost superhuman to become a blue.' Her eyes travelled over his broad chest and muscled arms, not so concealed now that he was wearing only a close-fitting shirt, and she imagined the whipcord strength that he held in such close containment. Her eyes moved up to his face and she saw that he was watching her in open amusement.

Immediately her cheeks suffused with colour and Carlo laughed. 'You blush very easily, don't you?'

'It's the bane of my life,' Petra admitted with a sigh. 'I can't wait to grow out of it.'

'Don't be in such a hurry. It's most attractive.' He spoke lightly, but Petra thought that he was funning her again and turned away to look at some of the other photographs. 'Are these your relations?'

'Most of them.' He moved to stand just behind her and Petra found it strangely difficult to breathe when he was so near. When he started to tell her who the people in the frames were, she didn't listen, was only aware of his voice and a tingling sensation in the back of her neck that spread right down to her toes. She could smell his aftershave and almost feel his breath on her hair. At the same time she became terribly aware of her own body, of her own sexuality, and she felt an overpowering need to touch Carlo. A need so strong that she was sure he must sense it. All she had to do was to step back a little, just a few inches, and their bodies would touch. Petra wanted that very badly, but upbringing, inexperience, shyness, a fear of a rebuff all held her back. And then the moment was gone because Carlo moved down the room to point out another photograph further along. Petra followed him numbly, but this time stood further away, keeping a safe distance between them.

When he'd gone through the photographs, he poured more drinks and said, 'I seem to remember that you said you'd left some of your things in the left luggage department at the Gare Austerlitz. If you'll let me have the ticket I'll arrange to have them collected for you.' Which was a very tactful way of saying that he was fed up with seeing her in the same dress, Petra thought ruefully as she handed the ticket over.

Tony came early and Petra hurried out into the hall

to meet him. They left at once, without Tony seeing
Carlo, and although Tony was a little withdrawn at
first, he soon melted when she smiled and let him see
how glad she was to be with him. He took her to a fish
restaurant near the Rialto where she didn't feel out of
place in her shirtwaister, and when the food and wine
had worked their effect, they laughed and talked
happily together, perfectly at ease in each other's
company. To Petra it was a relief to be with him, and to
feel calm and comfortable, not nervous and restless as
she was with Carlo. She knew exactly where she was
with Tony, he was just like her brother's friends, the
boys she knew from the tennis club, or the sons of
neighbours and her parents' friends. A few years older,
certainly, and more widely travelled and experienced,
but basically with the same standards and values. And
she knew what to expect from him and what he wanted
from her. She knew that he would take her out a few
times before he made a pass and just how far to let him
go before she said no. She knew what to wear when she
went out with him and what subjects to discuss without
getting into a heated argument. But with Carlo
everything was different. And it wasn't only because he
was a foreigner, brought up in a different world; there
was something about him that deprived her of common
sense, of the thin veneer of sophistication that her small
experience of life had given her. Every time she was
with him she'd felt nervous and on edge. Which was
probably why he found her so amusing, guessing that
she was so inexperienced that she found him
overpoweringly masculine.

'Penny for them,' Tony said wryly, breaking into her
thoughts.

'Oh, sorry.' She realised that she hadn't heard a word
he'd said in the last five minutes. 'It was something you

said earlier; it made me remember an incident like that that happened to my father.' And she was able to pass off her lack of concentration.

'How about tomorrow night?' Tony asked as he walked her back to the palazzo. 'Or has Berini got something planned for you?'

'No, he hasn't mentioned anything.'

Petra was going to add that she'd like to check with Carlo, but Tony said quickly, 'Good, I'll pick you up at the same time, then.' And before she could speak pushed her gently back against the wall of the deserted alleyway and kissed her. This time he showed more passion; not the open-mouthed thrusting tongue kind of an inexperienced boy, but the deep compulsion of a man. An embrace from which Petra surfaced breathlessly several minutes later. He went on kissing her for some time until Petra gently pushed him away and said, 'Hey, I'd better go in. I don't want to get Maria out of bed on my first day.'

He was very reluctant to let her go, but she at last managed to persuade him and rang the bell. But it was Carlo who came to the door, not Maria. He gave a brief nod to Tony, who said unnecessarily, 'Till tomorrow night then, darling.'

Carlo closed the door behind her and Petra walked through ahead of him into the outer hall and went across to the stairs, pausing at their foot. 'I'm sorry if I kept you up.'

'You didn't.' His eyes went over her and Petra wished he wouldn't; she knew that her hair was untidy and that she didn't have any lipstick left on. 'But I should have remembered to give you a key. Here.' He felt in his pocket and held one out to her, 'I looked this out for you earlier.'

'Thank you.' She walked back across the hall and

took the key from his outstretched hand, but her own
was shaking so much that she dropped it.

Carlo bent to retrieve it for her and again put it into
her hand. 'You're shaking,' he said in surprise. Then,
dryly, 'Signor Reid seems to have quite an effect on
you. He must be very experienced.'

'Oh, he isn't. I mean, I don't ...' Petra blushed
furiously, saw the mockery in his eyes and her cheeks
went immediately pale again. 'I'm very tired. If you'll
excuse me, I'll go to bed,' she said with as much dignity
as she could gather.

'Of course. But I wanted to tell you that I shall be
going to Padua tomorrow and shall leave quite early so
probably won't see you. But please ask Maria for
anything you want.'

'Thank you. That's very kind of you. Have—have a
good journey,' she said stiffly.

'Thank you.' Reaching out, he took hold of her left
hand and carried it to his lips, his eyes on her face. He
kissed it very lightly although his grip was strong.
'Good night, Petra.'

He left at six the next morning, but Petra hadn't slept
very well and was at her window to watch him go. He
was wearing a dark suit and Petra wondered if he was
going on business or whether he was going to meet
Francesca. The day suddenly seemed to stretch long
and empty in front of her, even though she was going to
see Tony again that night. She ate breakfast alone in
a small room overlooking the garden, and all attempts
to make conversation with Maria failed dismally.
Dejectedly she wandered the streets, showing round her
photo of Sara with the same glaring lack of success. At
lunchtime, sitting in a café and making pizza and a
drink last as long as she could, Petra suddenly made up
her mind and asked to use their telephone, putting a

call through to Peter Dudley in Paris to ask his advice about trying to contact Sara's parents. He agreed with her that they couldn't put if off any longer and promised to put the matter in hand. It was a decision that had been haunting Petra for days and to have made it was a great relief, even if it meant having to accept that to go on searching for Sara in Venice was now largely a waste of time. She had done all she could, but even with the help of Carlo and the Consulate there had been no real trace of her, nothing that would help to find her.

When she got back to her room in the Palazzo Petra found that her other suitcase had arrived from Paris; not only arrived but Maria had pressed all her clothes and hung them up for her. Gratefully she ran downstairs to the kitchen to tell the housekeeper how much she appreciated it, but Maria brusquely waved away her thanks. 'El Conte, he expect me to do it.'

'I see. Well, thank you anyway.'

'You eat here?' Maria asked with scarcely concealed hostility.

'No, I'm going out to dinner,' Petra replied defiantly, glad that she was able to say it.

And it was gratifying to have Tony tell her how lovely she looked when he came to call for her. 'I'm glad you like it; it's a dress I haven't worn before.'

'A new one?'

'Oh, no. I left most of my things in Paris but Carlo had them brought to Venice for me, so I'm able to wear something different at last.'

'Lucky Carlo to have so much influence,' Tony said with cool derision.

Petra turned to look into his face. 'You don't like him, do you?'

Tony shrugged. 'Not much. He puts my back up.'

'I don't see why. He's only trying to help.'

Putting an arm round her shoulders, Tony drew her closer. 'Forget about Berini,' he said dismissively. 'Where would you like to eat?'

Their evening was spent much the same as the previous one, but several times Petra found her thoughts wandering and had to consciously pull herself together to concentrate on what Tony was saying. Towards the end of the meal he noticed it too. 'Hey, you're miles away!'

'Sorry, Tony.' She blinked and sat up straighter. 'It's just tiredness. I didn't sleep very well last night.'

'Because you were thinking of me, I hope.'

'Of course.' Petra smiled at him. 'That and the strange surroundings, I expect.'

After Tony had paid the bill and they'd left the restaurant, he put an arm round her waist and said, 'If you're tired you won't want to walk around like we did last night, so how about going back to my flat for a nightcap?'

Petra felt strangely reluctant, but didn't much want to wander round the city again either. 'Is it far?' she temporised.

'Only a few hundred yards. We'll be there in just a few minutes.'

It was a pleasant flat, on the third floor of a decent old house near the Strada Nuova, with just a bedroom, sitting-room, tiny kitchen and bathroom. And it was very much a bachelor flat, the only personal things on display being books and a few pictures.

'It's nice,' Petra remarked looking round. 'Did you have much difficulty finding it?'

'It came with the job. One flat; consular official for the use of. When I move on someone else from the Consulate will take it over.'

'Are you likely to move on soon?'

'In about nine months I expect. Hopefully to an embassy in an equally pleasant city.' He gave her a drink and said, 'Come and sit here with me on the settee.' Petra did so and he moved up close, putting an arm across her shoulders. 'I've been invited to the Independence Day ball at the American Consulate this weekend. Would you like to come along with me?'

'Is that allowed?' Petra asked in surprise.

'I can arrange it. It's a formal occasion, though. You'd have to wear evening dress, although it doesn't have to be a long dress, if you see what I mean?'

'Thanks. I'd love to go. And I do have something to wear now that my case has arrived.'

'Good.' Tony leant forward and kissed her shoulder, then took her glass from her and put it aside before taking her in his arms and kissing her properly. 'Darling, you're so sweet.' His kisses became more passionate and he pushed her back against the end of the settee, his hands pushing aside the straps of her dress so that he could free her breasts. Petra responded at first, but somehow it wasn't the same and she couldn't lose herself in his embrace.

'I ought to go.'

'No, not yet.' His hands gripped her shoulders and Tony buried his face in her neck, kissing her fiercely until she pulled away. He drew back, putting a hand under her chin so that he could kiss her mouth again. 'Petra, oh Petra, you're so wonderful,' he murmured thickly against her mouth, his hand again going to her breast. And when she tried to resist, 'Relax, darling. I only want to touch you. I won't do anything you don't like.'

So Petra let him fondle her again. After all it wasn't as if this had never happened to her before. There had been other boys that she'd gone this far with; it was nothing really, and she liked Tony. But suddenly she broke away from him again and stood up, pulling her dress into place. 'I'd like to leave now, please.'

Tony gave a groaning sigh, then resignedly got to his feet. 'Okay, don't panic. I'll take you home.' Putting his hands on her shoulders, he looked into her face and said, 'Are you a virgin, Petra?'

Her face flushed. 'Mind your own damn . . .'

'All right. All right.' He put up a hand to stop her. 'It's just that—well, I've really fallen for you, Petra. And you turn me on. So much that I don't want to let you go.' He kissed her, his mouth insinuating and said softly, 'Stay with me, darling. Please stay.'

'No. No, I can't.' She looked at him with troubled eyes. 'I'm sorry, Tony. I like you, but . . .'

'But I'm going too fast for you. Okay, I'll be patient. But if two people like each other enough.' He shrugged, then grinned and said, 'And if you only knew what you do to me.'

As he walked her home, Petra chided herself for having been so abrupt and silly. It wouldn't have hurt her to go on letting him kiss her, especially when she liked him so much and he had been so kind to her. But she hadn't been able to be a part of his lovemaking and that had felt all wrong. It could only be tiredness; she'd had so little sleep last night and the night before none at all because she had been watching the dawn with Carlo. Her thoughts went back to that one kiss on the boat which she had never wanted to end, but she shook the memory angrily aside. How could she think of one man when she was with another? It was ridiculous.

'We shouldn't have to get anyone out of bed tonight,' Tony remarked as they came to the door of the palazzo. 'It isn't all that late.'

'It's all right, Carlo gave me a key.'

Tony wouldn't let her go without kissing her, his mouth again passionate, and Petra made herself respond so that he went home happy, promising to call for her on the following Saturday.

There was a light on in the inner hall when she let herself in, but the outer hall was lit only by the soft light from the top of the stairs. Petra guessed that Carlo wasn't home yet and Maria had just left her enough light to find her way to her room. If Carlo was coming home at all. Maybe he was spending the night in Padua with Francesca. She pushed the thought and the pictures that came with it out of her mind and strode across the hall towards the stairs, her high heels echoing on the marble floors. But as she passed the library the door opened and Carlo came out into the hall. So he wasn't with Francesca! A surge of satisfaction filled her, so fierce that it left her breathless and she could only stand and stare at him.

'It's all right,' he said quickly, mistaking her stillness for fear. 'It's Carlo.'

'Yes.' She turned and walked slowly towards him. 'You finished your business in Padua, then?' And when he nodded. 'I'm glad.'

Raising his eyebrows a little, Carlo stood aside to let her go into the library. 'Would you like a drink?'

She shook her head. 'No, not really.' She smiled at him, feeling inexplicably happy.

'Did you have a good evening?'

'It was okay.'

'But you're glad I'm back?'

'Yes,' she answered simply.

His eyes smiled at her. 'Now why can that be, I wonder?' He started to move towards her. 'Is it because you're afraid to be here at night without a man to protect you?' He came up close, looking down at her with devils in his eyes. 'Or is it because you missed me—just a little?' He put his hands on her shoulders and Petra's heart began to race so much she could hardly breathe. She lifted her head, lips parted, urgent for his kiss. But then his hands tightened and his face grew cold. Letting her go, he said grimly, 'You'd better go to bed. You must be tired.'

Turning away, he filled up his glass and sat down by the unlit fire, picking up a book that he'd been reading, shutting her out.

'Carlo?'

But he didn't look round, merely said, 'Good night.'

It wasn't until she'd undressed and went into the bathroom that Petra understood why he had suddenly become withdrawn. Looking into the mirror she saw that her lipstick was smudged, an obvious sign that she and Tony had been kissing. Oh hell! For a moment she felt a flash of anger at Tony, but was immediately contrite. He had every reason to expect to kiss her after she'd gone back to his flat with him, but Petra wished now that she hadn't gone; she hadn't really wanted to in the first place but there had been nowhere else to go and no real reason not to.

She sighed, realising that Tony was extremely jealous of Carlo, presumably because Carlo had so much compared to him. Although there was no reason to be jealous as far as she was concerned, of course. Or was there? Petra stared at herself in the mirror, wondering if Tony knew her better than she knew herself. It was true that Carlo excited her, and there was no denying that she found him terrifically attractive, when she was near him she wanted to touch and be touched, and she didn't feel at all like that with Tony. With Carlo she felt like a piece of metal drawn towards a powerful magnet, with no resistance to stay away. But to let these feelings matter, to let them develop into anything more would be fatal, because they would be purely one-sided. Petra had no illusions that Carlo would ever fall in love with her, even though it amused him to flirt and arouse her sexuality. Look at tonight for example; when she'd told him she was glad to see him, he'd been ready to flirt with her, but had changed completely when he realised that she had come straight from the arms of another man.

That thought made her feel suddenly dirty, even though she and Tony had hardly done more than exchange a few kisses, so she stood under the shower for much longer than necessary, washing herself until she felt clean again.

She didn't sleep too badly that night and in the morning had breakfast with Carlo, being careful to keep the conversation light and meaningless. Luckily Carlo seemed to fall into her mood, and in the afternoon took her for a trip to some of the islands around Venice in his motorboat. At Murano they visited a glass factory where he was met by the manager with great deference and glasses of champagne. Carlo insisted on buying her a glass bird, its wings outspread, that she said reminded her of his hawks, and the manager gave her a copy of one of the famous horses on top of St Mark's Church, which the glassblower made for her while she watched. Then they went to the tiny island of San Francesco del Deserto to visit the monastery there, its beautiful gardens tended by Franciscan friars, before going on to Burano, which Petra liked best. This, again, was a small island, which from a distance looked drunk because its tallest building, a campanile similar to that in St Mark's Square, was tilted over so much that it looked as if it might fall at any minute. Closer in, Petra saw that all the square little houses were painted in a glorious array of colours: blue, red, green, russet, all mixed up together, giving a charming effect. Carlo moored on the waterfront and they strolled up cobbled streets where women sat outdoors working on delicate pillow lace and fishermen sailed right up the little canals and moored by their front doors, mending their nets on their own doorsteps. Unlike Murano, which was heavily commercialised, or the monastery where they had been given wine, in Burano they found a pleasant outdoor café and Carlo bought them both coffee.

Petra laughed at him. 'Surely nothing less than champagne will do? Are you always given drinks wherever you go?'

'Only when they think I might buy something,' he answered dryly.

'But there was nothing to buy at the monastery, so they must love you for yourself,' she said flippantly.

Carlo smiled rather grimly. 'No, only for the donation they expect from me every Easter.'

Petra looked at him, wondering what it must be like to be so rich that people attached themselves to you like leeches, eager only for money. 'Don't you mind?'

He glanced at her quickly, then shook his head. 'I'm used to it. The Berinis have been supporting the monastery for the last five hundred years, and the glassworks has been under my family's patronage for almost as long. It's the obligation of the nobility to help the poor and the arts.'

'But surely it's the obligation of everyone who can afford it?'

'Of course. But I believe that nowadays they mostly depend on American and Japanese tourists, especially the glassworks,' he told her with a grin.

They had been going to go on to Torcello, but Petra liked Burano so much that they wandered round the island all over again, and then it was time to go back to Venice.

'Have you another date with Signor Reid?' Carlo asked on the way back.

'No, I'm not seeing him until Saturday. He's taking me to a ball at the American Consulate,' she felt compelled to add.

'Is he, indeed?' Carlo looked at her reflectively. 'Yes, I remember something about it. Then perhaps you'd like to have dinner with me tonight?'

He took her to the Danieli, near the Doge's Palace, and Petra wore her newest cream silk dress with a halter neck that looked good with her tan. But any half-formed hopes she might have had of being alone with Carlo evaporated when they ran into another couple who were friends of his and they all joined together for the evening, ending up at the famous Harry's Bar until the small hours.

Petra slept late the next morning while Carlo worked with his secretary in his study, but later in the afternoon he took her to the Ca' Rezzonico, a beautiful palazzo that had been kept exactly as it was in the eighteenth century, and where the poet Robert Browning had died. Petra had thought that the Palazzo Berini was beautiful but the Rezzonico was so magnificently decorated that it took her breath away and she got a crick in her neck from walking along looking up at the painted ceilings.

Carlo had a dinner engagement that evening so Petra ate alone in the breakfast room where Maria had set her a place, making it obvious that she didn't think Petra good enough for the dining-room. The rest of the evening she spent washing her hair and making sure that her clothes were ready for the ball tomorrow.

In Venice the only taxis are water taxis, so Petra had no choice but to walk to the American Consulate when Tony called for her the next day. She was wearing her 'femme fatale number' as Sara had always called it: a long black dress with thin gold chains for the shoulder straps and a matching gold belt. Usually she wore her sequined jacket over it, but as Sara had taken that with her, Petra had to make do with a long gold stole over her shoulders.

'Wow!' Tony's eyes widened in admiration when he saw her. 'You look stunning. I'm going to have to fight everyone else off.'

Petra laughed, but she knew she looked pretty good, and rather wished that Carlo had seen her before she left, but he had been nowhere around. The ballroom at the American Consulate was already crowded when they arrived and stood in line to be presented to their host and hostess. She had never seen so many bejewelled women in her life, every woman there seemed to be loaded with precious stones, and she felt almost undressed with only the gold gypsy bracelets and watch that she'd had for her twenty-first birthday. Her eyes feasted on the women's dresses, falling for some, hating others, but then Tony took her over to meet some of his colleagues and their wives and then asked her to dance.

'Enjoying yourself?' he asked, already certain that she was.

'Mm, it's great,' she answered enthusiastically. 'Are all the official functions you have to go to like this?'

'No, this is one of the more enjoyable parties. Usually you just stand around and drink and talk. Pretty boring, really.'

She laughed. 'I can't believe that.'

The walls were lined with mirrors, making the room

seem double its size and it was fun to watch the
colourfully dressed women and the men in their
evening suits, many of them with white tuxedos instead
of the more formal black. Tony was wearing one, too,
and he looked good in it. He was obviously enjoying
himself and held her possessively as they danced.
They had a drink and were dancing again when there
was a stir among the people standing on the edge of
the floor and heads turned to the doorway where the
Consul and his wife were coming into the room
accompanied by their guests of honour. Petra glimpsed
them in a mirror and stood rock still so that Tony
stumbled over her feet. He muttered an apology; but
Petra wasn't listening, her head whipped round and
she stared at the wide, arched entrance. Carlo was
standing beside the Consul's wife, terribly good
looking in his beautifully cut evening suit. As if
attracted by her gaze, he looked round and saw her,
then gave her a very definite wink.

'You didn't tell me he was coming.' Tony's annoyed
voice cut through her absorption and brought her
attention back to him.

'I didn't know. He didn't tell me either.'

They danced on but it was obvious that Tony was
angry, although Petra rather enjoyed the surprise. Carlo
danced with the Consul's wife, giving her his full
attention, and Petra didn't see him again until she was
standing with Tony and some other British guests and
he came up and asked her to dance. She felt Tony make
a movement of protest, but she just said, 'Of course,'
and put her hand in Carlo's as he led her on to the
floor.

It was a slow number and he held her quite loosely,
smiling lazily down at her. 'Surprised?'

'Very. Why didn't you tell me you were coming?'

'I wasn't sure that I was. One gets invited to so many of these sort of occasions.'

'Oh, one does,' Petra agreed in mocking pomposity.

Carlo laughed aloud, so that several people turned their heads to look. 'Minx. You haven't shown me your claws before.'

'Did you think I hadn't any?' Petra asked innocently, her eyes dancing.

'In that dress,' Carlo observed, his eyes running over her in open appreciation, 'I'm willing to believe you're capable of anything.'

'Anything?' she asked coquettishly.

'And everything,' he agreed, drawing her closer.

Petra was flirting with him and she knew it, but it was fun, that was all. She knew that Carlo didn't mean anything by it, that he was merely giving her as much attention as he had to the Consul's wife or any other woman he danced with; probably he'd flirted with her, too, but on a much more sophisticated level of course. At the end of the dance he took her back to Tony and she rather defiantly introduced him to the people she was with. Tony stayed silent but Carlo chatted to them until the next dance started and then excused himself.

Making little attempt to hide his annoyance, Tony took her on to the dance floor again and said, 'Did you have to dance with him?'

'Of course I did. He's my host.'

'You could have made an excuse.' Petra didn't answer and after a few moments he went on, 'I suppose you've been seeing quite a bit of him in the last few days?'

'He took me on a couple of sightseeing trips, yes.' He looked as if he was going to ask more questions, so Petra hastily launched into a lengthy description of

Burano that managed to divert him until the music ended.

Not wanting to annoy Tony further, Petra tried to give him all her attention and not look to see what Carlo was doing, but it was difficult not to watch when she caught sight of him in the mirror or when she looked over Tony's shoulder and saw him dancing nearby. Several times their eyes met, and held, until the turn of the music drew them away. At suppertime she and Tony sat with the rest of the guests from the British Consulate while Carlo went into another room with their hosts and the other guests of honour, but afterwards he came to claim her for another dance.

'I'm tired of making polite conversation,' he told her. 'Let's leave and take my boat over to the Lido, go for a moonlight swim.'

He was teasing of course, but Petra wistfully pictured it. 'Tony would never speak to me again if I did,' she answered, trying to keep her voice light.

'And would that break your heart?'

'Of course. A woman can't afford to throw over a perfectly eligible boyfriend you know. There aren't that many of them around.'

Carlo laughed. 'We mustn't do anything to alienate him then, must we?' But immediately belied his words by drawing her close and dancing with their bodies together, her hand held against his chest; much, much closer than he had danced with any other woman that evening.

The music ended, he loosened his hold and Petra moved to walk back to Tony, but Carlo kept hold of her hand. 'Don't go.' There was something in his voice that made her turn and look at him intently. 'Stay with me.' She read the message in his eyes and her heart gave a dizzying lurch—and she stayed.

When the music started they danced again. 'You're in a devilish mood tonight,' Petra told him, unable to resist laughing up at him.

'Maybe you bring out the devil in me,' he grinned back.

It was a fast beat number and they let themselves go, apart, but hardly aware of the other dancers as they twisted and swayed to the music. Carlo was good, really good, and Petra loved every minute, the full skirt of her dress swirling to reveal her shapely ankles and legs as she danced. At the end he caught her to him, laughing as he held her, both of them a little breathless. They were near the edge of the floor, on the far side of the room from Tony and the others, and with a lifted finger Carlo beckoned over a waiter with a tray of drinks.

'Mm, champagne again,' Petra said as the bubbles tickled her nose. 'What a way to live.'

'Perhaps you'd like me to drink some out of your shoe,' Carlo suggested, slipping an arm round her waist.

'You'd have a job, my shoes are nothing but a couple of straps. Look.' And she lifted her skirt a little to show him her foot.

'I hoped you'd do that,' Carlo said incorrigibly. 'Do you know you have very sexy ankles?'

Petra gurgled with laughter as he took her glass from her and pulled her into his arms to dance another slow one. Out of the corner of her eye she saw Tony move to come towards them and then turn back when he saw them start to dance, and she knew that people were watching them, noticing that they had danced three times in a row. But they weren't allowed to dance together long, because when they reached the other side of the floor Tony came up to them and said belligerently, 'This is my dance—and my partner.'

Carlo turned to look at him, that lazy smile again

curving his lips, and Tony drew himself up as if he was ready to fight. But Carlo only said, 'Of course,' and passed her over to Tony, merely giving her a nod before walking calmly away.

Petra let out a long breath of relief, afraid that Tony might have created a scene which wouldn't only have been nasty for them all but might have cost Tony his job. They danced around in a grim kind of silence and afterwards he kept a firm hold on her arm as they went back to join his friends, several of whom gave her speculative and rather cold looks. Later, when the others got up to dance, they sat alone on a small settee tucked away into a corner.

'Did you have to damn well make an exhibition of yourself?' Tony demanded furiously.

'We were only dancing . . .' Petra began mildly.

'For over half an hour!'

'I'm sorry, but you could have danced with someone else.'

'I did. But you were so taken up with Berini you didn't even notice!' Which was so true that Petra could find nothing to say. Tony, too, was silent for a few moments, then burst out, 'Don't you know what he's like? He's just a rich playboy, a womaniser. Dancing with you like that has convinced everyone here that he intends to have an affair with you—if he isn't already having one,' Tony added bitterly.

Her face white, Petra stood up. 'There's really no point in staying is there?'

Catching her wrist, Tony pulled her back into her seat. 'We'll stay until I'm ready to go. What's the matter, can't you wait to get back to go to bed with him?'

Petra wrenched her wrist free, gave him a fulminating look and strode quickly away to the ladies' cloakroom to collect her stole. When she came out Tony was waiting for her, but she ignored him and walked past him out of the building. He came after her and tried to take her arm but she shook him off. 'Leave me alone. Go back to the dance.'

'I can't let you walk home alone. You're going the wrong way,' he added as she went to turn into an alley leading from a square. 'It's that way.'

They walked in silence for several minutes, then Tony said, 'Look, I'm sorry. I know I shouldn't have said that but I was mad and—and damned jealous, if you must know. I care about you and I didn't enjoy seeing you being made a fool of by a man like Berini.'

'He wasn't making a fool of me.'

He laughed harshly. 'You were making a fool of yourself, then.'

'Yes,' Petra answered steadily, 'I suppose I was.'

'Do you know what you're saying?'

Petra turned to look at him, all her doubts suddenly resolving into certainties. 'Yes, I think so.'

Tony stared back at her. 'He's no good for you, Petra. He'll never marry you,' he said urgently.

'No. I didn't ever suppose that he would.'

'But you're going to go ahead with it?'

She shook her head. 'I don't know that I'm going to go ahead with anything. I only know how I feel.'

'You'll get hurt.'

'Perhaps. Perhaps not. It doesn't really matter.'

'I see.' They walked on to the entrance to the alleyway leading to the palazzo. His voice harsh, Tony said, 'I wish we'd met before, back in England. Or any other time but now.' Petra nodded but didn't speak. 'If you need help or if you change your mind, you know where to find me.'

'Thank you. But I won't do that.'

He seemed about to say something more, then turned abruptly on his heel and hurried away.

Petra let herself into the palazzo and went into the library to wait for Carlo to come home.

CHAPTER EIGHT

SHE didn't have long to wait, he was there within twenty minutes. Hardly long enough for her to find a bottle of champagne and a couple of cut glass flutes and set them out on the table ready. His eyes went swiftly to her face, and then he smiled. 'Are we celebrating something?' he asked, as she handed him the bottle of champagne.

'Of course. The fourth of July.'

'And why should a Venetian and an Englishwoman—especially an Englishwoman—want to celebrate American Independence day?'

'Because today is a very special day.'

The cork flew off and Carlo hastily caught the erupting liquid in one of the glasses, then handed it to her. 'I'll drink to that.' He filled his own glass and clinked it against hers. 'To today.' And added something in Italian that she didn't understand and he didn't translate. They drank, their eyes holding. 'No trouble with the boyfriend?' Carlo asked. 'I was worried when I saw him going after you, but I couldn't get away immediately.'

'No, no trouble. And no boyfriend any more.'

He grinned satanically. 'It worked, then?'

'He's the jealous type,' Petra agreed, knowing exactly what he meant.

'So I thought.' Putting down his glass he moved to come up behind her, his hands on her waist. 'You look very lovely tonight.' He bent to lightly kiss her shoulder. 'Do you forgive me?'

167

Petra let out a slow exhalation of breath as his lips moved up towards her neck. 'Yes, I forgive you.'

'Did I ever tell you you have beautiful shoulders?' he asked, lifting his hands to gently stroke them.

'No, but I believe you did mention my ankles.'

There was amusement in his voice as he said, 'Mmm, very sexy. And gorgeous legs, too.' His lips moved up the column of her neck.

'How do you know what my legs look like?' Petra said unsteadily, her breath catching in her throat.

'I've seen you in shorts, remember?'

'You didn't say that my legs looked gorgeous at the time.'

'There's a time and a place for everything.' His lips moved to her ear, bit gently at the lobe. 'This is a sensational dress,' he murmured in her ear and began to slide his finger gently down the edge of the halter.

Her nerves suddenly returning, Petra answered at random, too aroused to think straight. 'I bought it in London before we came to Paris. I thought we would be going out to really with-it places, but we hardly got an opportunity to go anywhere so I never wore it.' Carlo's finger went further down and she gasped. 'It—it should have a jacket with multi-coloured sequins to go with it, but Sara took that with her so I had to wear a stole tonight, but I . . .'

She broke off as Carlo turned her round to face him, his dark eyes intent on her mouth. He bent nearer and moved his lips gently, exploringly over hers. Petra closed her eyes, lost to everything but his kiss. But her eyes flew open again as he moved away and a second later said, '*What* did you say?'

'Huh?' Petra stared at him uncomprehendingly.

'Just now. You said something about a sequin.'

'What?' For a moment she couldn't think straight.

'Oh, yes. I said I had a sequinned jacket to go with this dress.' She couldn't think why on earth he wanted to know, why he'd stopped kissing her just because of that.

'With multi-coloured sequins? And you gave it to Sara?'

'Yes, that's right. But I don't . . .'

'Come with me.' Grabbing her hand, Carlo ran with her out into the hall and up the stairs, along the corridor and pushed open the door of his bedroom, Petra holding up her skirts so that she could keep up with him.

'Hey, now wait a minute!' Petra thought that she might have been taken to his room that night, but certainly not in this all-fired hurry.

'Look.' Carlo crossed to the chest of drawers, opened the top one and took out a beautiful leather stud box. 'I found this in the bottom of one of the wardrobes in here some time ago and meant to ask Maria about it, but it went out of my head.' He held out his finger. Resting on it was a small, round, multi-coloured sequin.

Petra stared, open-mouthed. 'In—in your wardrobe? When did you find it?'

'It was after I came back from America. I don't use that particular wardrobe, just keep suitcases in there. And I noticed the sequin when I went to put the empty case back.'

'It wasn't there before you left?'

'I didn't see it, no.'

Petra tried hard not to get too excited, too hopeful. 'Could it have been left by someone who stayed here, someone who hung their clothes in that cupboard? Francesca or somebody?'

Putting a finger under her chin, Carlo lifted her face

so that she looked directly at him. 'Francesca has never been inside my bedroom.'

'Oh.'

'Quite.' And he leant forward to kiss her on the mouth.

Slowly, reluctantly, Petra came back to reality when he at last lifted his head. 'And you think Maria might know how the sequin got there? Shall we—shall we ask her?'

'She isn't here, I gave her the night off. We'll have to wait until she comes in the morning.'

'So long?'

'So long,' he agreed and bent to kiss her again. 'Why don't we finish that champagne in bed?' he breathed softly. 'I'll get it.'

He was back before she'd even had time to unpin her hair and let it fall about her shoulders. He shut the door firmly behind him and came to finish the task for her, running his hands through her hair as she turned towards him. He undressed her slowly, his eyes revelling in the velvet smoothness of her skin, his caressing hands sending tremors of sexuality running through her. 'Your turn now,' he whispered when there were no clothes left to take off, and she slowly obeyed him, her hands uncertain where his had been sure. His body was beautiful, to touch and to look at, but she was shy when he drew her close and held her against him. '*Cara,*' he whispered. '*Ho tanto bisogno di te.*' Then he bent and left a searing trail of kisses down her body until Petra gasped and tried to pull away. But he held her shuddering body until she gave an inarticulate moan and her fingers curled fiercely in his hair.

Picking her up, Carlo carried her swiftly to the big bed and laid her down on the soft white sheets, looking down at her for a moment, deep desire in his eyes, before lying down beside her.

The weight of Carlo's arm lay across her when Petra woke the next morning. It was early, the sun still pale through the shutters, and she hadn't slept long, but she felt no tiredness even though her body ached in places. She felt terrifically, wonderfully, elatedly happy, and felt that she must somehow try and hold this moment for ever. Carefully she turned so that she could look at him. He was asleep still, his face softened in repose, his mouth curved as if he was smiling at his dreams. He had taught her many things last night, things about herself and her body's capacity for pleasure that she'd never known before. And he had taught her how to give pleasure, too, but in an unselfish way so that it was a joy for them both. And he had murmured many wonderful things, of his delight in her body, of how beautiful he found her. But when passion took him to the heights of ecstasy, then he could only groan out his feelings in Italian so that she didn't understand the words, but only what he did. And that, too, was very, very wonderful.

Shyly almost, Petra pushed back the thin sheet that covered them so that she could see his outline in the muted sunlight. His chest was mostly smooth with very few hairs, and he was tanned from long hours in the sun. Very gently she reached out to run her fingers lightly along the swelling muscles of his arm, then across his shoulder and down his chest, lingering over the nipple, and then on down to his waist and the flat plane of his stomach before taking her hand away.

But as she did so, Carlo reached out and caught it. 'Why stop there?' he said huskily and replaced her hand, then leaned nearer to kiss her. 'Now make love to me,' he said only minutes later and drew her down on top of him.

Later she again lay beside him, spent and breathless, her body silken with perspiration, her hair clinging to her neck and forehead. 'Oh, Carlo.' She clung to him, her body trembling, and his arms tightened round her. Silly tears gathered in her eyes but she blinked them away.

'What is it, *cara*?' He gently pushed the hair off her forehead.

'Nothing. I just—just never felt like this before, that's all.' Petra bit her lip, determined not to get serious, not to let her feelings show. With a choking laugh, she said, 'Do you make all your women feel like this?'

An angry look came into Carlo's dark eyes. '*All* my women? Just what kind of . . .' His voice broke off as they heard the street door open and close and footsteps cross the hall. 'That's Maria.'

'The sequin!' Her eyes stared into his.

Carlo pushed back the sheet. 'I'll shower and go and talk to her.'

When he'd gone into the bathroom Petra pulled the sheet off the bed and wrapped it round her like a toga, then gathered up her clothes. At the door, she glanced back at the bed, but there was no hiding the fact that they had slept together from Maria or anyone. The gallery was empty so she ran along it and up the stairs to her own room, showering and changing as quickly as she could. But Carlo was already talking to Maria, she could hear their voices coming from the kitchen and pushed open the door to go in. They were talking in Italian of course, but it was obvious from Maria's scared look that she knew something.

An hour later the three of them were on their way to the police station in Carlo's boat. Maria was sniffing

into her handkerchief now although she'd wept quite a
lot when Carlo had forced her to admit that when she
returned to the palazzo after her visit to her sister's she
had found that Carlo's bed had been slept in, and a lot
of the food and drink was missing, so that it was
obvious someone had not only been there but had
stayed several days. When he had furiously demanded
to know why she hadn't told him, she had wept some
more and said that she had lost the keys while at her
sister's and not found them again until a couple of days
before she was due to return. Carlo had questioned her
more closely and then spent a long time on the phone to
the police, only translating it all to Petra while they
waited for the police to call them back and tell them to
come down to the station.

Maria began to cry again as they went in, especially
when she saw the surly young man that the police
officer was questioning. He stood up and hurled a
tirade of impassioned abuse at poor Maria until a
policeman got hold of him and pushed him down into
his chair again. The Inspecttore turned respectfully to
Carlo and went into a long explanation, waving his
hands a lot, then Carlo translated for her, his face grim.
'This man is Maria's nephew, Enrico. He works at the
garage where I have my car serviced—a job Maria
asked me to help him get incidentally. He knew I was
going to be away so when Maria was staying at his
mother's house he stole her set of keys to the palazzo,
then went joy-riding in my car to Paris, where he met
Sara. He brought her back here, pretending to be me,
and they stayed in the palazzo.' His face grew even
grimmer at the thought of the invasion of his home.

'And—and Sara!' Petra asked, hardly able to breathe.

'He says that she found out the truth because she
found a photograph of me. Then she didn't want to

know him any more and insisted on going back to
Paris. He says he took her to the station in my boat—
damn him to hell—and left her there.'

'He didn't go in with her? See her on to a train?'

'No, he just dropped her off at the station and went
straight back to the palazzo. To sleep in my bed again
and drink himself silly on my wine, I don't doubt,' he
added savagely.

But Petra was gazing blankly into space. 'So we're no
further forward. We still don't know what happened to
Sara.'

Carlo put his arm round her. 'No, but the police will
go on questioning him and if he's hiding anything
they'll find out.'

Leaving Maria at the police station, they went back
to the palazzo and Petra made breakfast. It was their
first meal alone together and it should have been a close
and wonderful one after last night, but they were both
subdued, Petra because there was not more news of
Sara, Carlo angry at his servant's carelessness and
disloyalty.

'Will you dismiss Maria?' Petra asked eventually.

'I already have. I don't want her back.'

'I suppose it wasn't entirely her fault,' she ventured.
'She probably only covered up for him for her sister's
sake.'

'Possibly, but it only made things worse.' He looked
at her, then reached out to take her hand and pulled her
on to his lap. 'I don't think I said good morning to you
earlier.'

Petra smiled. 'I don't think you did at that.'

'I must have had other things on my mind.' He kissed
her lingeringly and then sighed. 'I could do this all day.'

'So why don't we?' she murmured against his mouth.

'I want to.' He groaned and kissed her, but then

pushed her off his lap and stood up. 'It will have to be later, I'm afraid. I've had an idea that I want to follow up.'

'You're going out?'

'Yes, but I'll try not to be too long.' Taking her in his arms he kissed her hungrily, his hand inside her blouse, and it was quite a while before he released her. 'Will that do until I get back?' he asked huskily.

'Mmm.' Petra still had her arms around his neck as she slowly opened her eyes. 'But only if you hurry.' He laughed and she smiled with him, but then her expression grew serious. 'Carlo?'

'Yes.'

'You—you make me feel—wanton,' she said, her face troubled.

'No, I don't. I've just made your body come alive, that's all. I've made you feel like a woman.' Putting his hands low on her hips he held her close against his own body. 'Just as you make me feel like a man,' he said thickly, leaving her in no doubt about what he meant.

He left her then and Petra went up to his room to strip the bed and remake it, but it took her some time to find the clean sheets so she was still up there twenty minutes later when the bell on the Canal door of the palazzo reverberated through the house. Poking her head through a window, Petra saw a water-taxi at the steps, but couldn't see who was standing under the portico. Running downstairs, she opened the massive door, thinking how incongruous it was that someone should arrive in a boat.

Francesca stood on the doorstep, looking cool and elegant in a wine-coloured dress. For a moment Petra felt a stab of jealousy, but then remembered last night and drew herself up. 'Hallo, Francesca. Do come in, but I'm afraid Carlo isn't here.'

The other girl looked at her narrowly, then turned and said something to the taxi-driver so that the boat sped away. 'Thank you.' Francesca walked in. 'I would like a cool drink. Let us go into the library, shall we?' She walked ahead as if she owned the place, then sat down in a chair and left Petra to get the drinks. After she'd given her one, Petra sat down opposite and tried hard to remember that Carlo was only a friend of Francesca's, not her lover. He was *her* lover now, and although the thought brought a flush of colour to her cheeks, it helped a lot.

'Someone mentioned that Carlo had taken you in,' Francesca remarked, as if she were a stray dog or something. 'Didn't you have anywhere to go?'

'I expect I could have found somewhere,' Petra replied calmly. 'But Carlo insisted I stay here.'

'Really? He always did have an unnecessarily high standard of—responsibility, is that the correct word?' she asked in her charming Italian accent.

'I'm sure you know all the right words, Francesca,' Petra replied sweetly.

'But you don't speak any Italian at all, do you?'

'Not yet, no.'

The other girl looked at her pityingly. 'The English are hopeless at foreign languages; that's why they always expect other people to speak their own.' Petra didn't bother to answer and she put down her glass with a snap. 'It really wouldn't do to get any ideas about Carlo, you know, even though he took you to the ball.'

So gossip had got back to Francesca already. 'You're mistaken,' Petra said coolly. 'I was taken to the dance by a friend from the British Consulate.'

Francesca looked as if she didn't know whether to be pleased or not. 'But you danced with Carlo there?'

'Yes, I danced with him—several times,' she said, rubbing it in.

The other girl glared at her. 'You're his mistress, aren't you? You wouldn't be so confident if you were not.'

Petra flushed again but didn't attempt to deny it.

Francesca stood up. 'He will not marry you, you know. He is just amusing himself with you. You threw yourself at him and so he took you. But you need not think that he is serious. He would not marry such a one as you. He told me himself that he finds you amusing—funny.'

Her English had slipped a bit but she made herself quite clear. Petra gripped the arms of her chair and tried hard to keep her temper. She managed to say as steadily as she could, 'You're the second person who's said that to me. But as I've never believed that Carlo might want to marry me, it's all rather unnecessary, don't you think? And as you're not engaged to him yourself, I really don't feel that you have any right to come here and lecture me.'

Francesca was staring at her in surprise. 'You don't want to marry him? You are willing to settle for an affair?'

'I'm willing to settle for anything he cares to give.'

'You are interested only in his money, then. It is that that you want.'

'His money?' Petra looked at her and began to laugh. 'God, Francesca, where are your eyes? Carlo's money is the last thing I'm interested in.' And she was still laughing when Francesca walked huffily out of the room and left the palazzo.

Petra was sitting in the library reading a magazine when Carlo came back. He came straight over to put a hand on either arm of her chair and leaned down to kiss her long and lingeringly. 'Okay?' he asked softly.

'Mm. Fine.'

'Let's go out to lunch then, and then on to the lido.'

'Lovely.' Petra stood up. 'Was your idea any good?'

'Not really. I thought the men who worked at the station and who have been on holiday might have returned by now. Some of them had but they didn't remember seeing Sara. But there are a couple more who aren't due back until tomorrow.' He glanced round and saw the two empty glasses. 'Has Reid been here?' he asked sharply.

'No, it was Francesca. She called in to see you but when you weren't here just had a drink and left again.'

'Did she say what she wanted?'

Petra turned away so that he couldn't see her face. 'No, she didn't say.'

The lido was again crowded, but Carlo took her to the far end of the island, away from the public beaches, to a small villa he had there with its own private beach. And there, after they'd sunbathed, he took her inside and made love to her in the villa's shady bedroom, made love to her until her cries of pleasure dwindled to a soft sigh of his name. 'Oh, Carlo, Carlo, Carlo.'

It was already evening when they went back to the palazzo with the intention of changing and going out to dinner at the Cipriani, but while Petra was standing under the shower, Carlo came up behind her and took the soap from her, his hands tracing erotic patterns on her skin, so they didn't go out at all, but ended up with fruit and champagne in bed.

They slept late the next morning and were woken by the phone ringing beside the bed. Carlo answered it sleepily but sat up quickly, wide awake. Putting the phone down, he leant down and kissed her. 'I have to go out,' he murmured, gently biting her ear.

'Now?' Petra sighed with disappointment.

He laughed. 'I'm afraid so.' Getting out of bed he went into the bathroom.

'What about breakfast?'

'I'll grab a croissant on my way out,' he called above the purr of his electric razor. 'My secretary will be here soon; if you need anything just ask him.'

'Him? You have a male secretary?' She remembered how her jealous mind had run riot about that.

'Yes.' He came out and began to dress. 'Stay here till I get back, okay?'

Petra had pulled the sheet up to her chin and lifted her knees to rest her arms on them. 'You mean here in bed?'

Carlo grinned. 'You think it might save time?'

'Why, yes. And—it's where I belong, isn't it?'

He caught the unsteady note in her voice and came over, fully dressed now. 'It's certainly where I intend to spend a great deal of time with you. But why don't we discuss that when I get back?' He kissed the end of her nose. 'Be ready to go out, *si?*'

Petra smiled and put her arms round his neck. 'Okay, boss. Hurry back.'

When he'd gone she dressed and ate a leisurely breakfast, but had nothing to do when she'd tidied it away except to go into the drawing-room and watch the Canal. She felt in an ambiguous position, not a guest any more but not sure enough of herself to just take over the place and do the dusting or whatever. It was still early when the street doorbell rang and she ran to answer it, forestalling the secretary who poked his head out of Carlo's study. It was Tony. He stood on the doorstep, his face cold and withdrawn. 'Good morning.'

'Oh! H-hallo, Tony.'

'Might I come in for a moment? I'd like to talk to you.'

'If it's about the dance the other night ...'

'No. It's about Sara.'

Petra stared at him and moved slowly aside to let him in. He shut the door and said, 'Is Berini at home?'

'No, he had to go out. What—what is it about Sara?'

Tony hesitated. 'There's no easy way to tell you. A body has been found. We think it could be Sara.'

Petra had been half expecting something like this for weeks, but it still came as a shock and for a moment everything went black.

'Are you all right?' Tony grabbed her arm.

'Yes. Yes, I'm okay.' But her face was chalk white when Petra said, 'Where—where did you find her?'

'She was found a couple of miles from a station on the main line from Venice to Paris. The police think she may have been lured off the train and then killed.' Tony paused, then said awkwardly, 'I'm afraid they need you to make a positive identification.'

Petra's hands balled into tight fists. 'Yes, of course. I'll get my bag.' Somehow she got up to her room and remembered to look in on Carlo's secretary to tell him where she was going on the way back.

That journey, first by boat and then in a Consulate car, was the longest Petra had ever known. She didn't talk much, just asked Tony if Sara's passport or any other papers had been found with the body. He shook his head. 'No, everything she had must have been stolen.'

The police mortuary was very like a prison with a high wall and barred windows. Tony took her in and spoke to the policeman there, showing him his identification. Then the policeman took out a bunch of keys and led them down a long bare corridor, their footsteps echoing hollowly on the tiled floor. Like the caverns of the dead, Petra thought wildly, her feet faltering. Tony looked at her anxiously, the first time that he'd let any emotion show. 'Okay?' She nodded weakly and he said, 'It's better to get it over with quickly.'

The policeman unlocked a door at the end and pulled it open. It was a heavy door that clanged against the wall sending echoes through her head. Tony took her arm and, biting her lip hard, she moved into the room with him. There was a figure lying on a slablike table with a sheet over it. The policeman said something and Tony translated in a shaken voice. 'He—he says that she has been out in the open for some time.'

The man jerked the sheet back from the head of the blonde-haired corpse. Petra cried out in horror and revulsion. 'Oh, God!' Her hands went up to her mouth and she turned violently away.

'Is it Sara? Petra, we have to be sure. Is it Sara?'

But she couldn't speak, could only retch and struggle in his arms to get out of the room as he tried to hold her. They reached the door and then she heard her name in a great shout that reverberated down the echoing corridor.

'Carlo!' Pulling free from Tony she ran to him like an arrow going to the gold. He caught her and held her fiercely as she sobbed incoherently. 'Oh God, it was terrible. Oh, Carlo. They said it was Sara, but it wasn't. Oh, dear God.' She put her hand to her mouth and retched again.

Picking her up, Carlo carried her outside into the open, dumped her on a convenient seat and pushed her head down between her knees. 'Take deep breaths,' he commanded.

Dimly above her she could hear him talking fiercely to Tony, telling him exactly what he thought of him for bringing her here, and in English, too. She tried to sit up but he kept his hand on her head while Tony got the biggest strip torn off him he'd ever had in his life.

'Hey! Let me up, I'm all right now.'

Quickly he removed his hand. 'You're sure?'

'Yes. You forgot about me,' she said accusingly.

He smiled. 'But only for a moment, *cara*.' He helped her to her feet. 'Let's get back to Venice.'

'It wasn't Sara,' she said anxiously, half turning to go back to the police station. 'I'm not sure if I told Tony that.'

'Yes, you did. He knows. He's gone back to tell them.' He led her over to his red Ferrari parked at the kerb, the door still open from when he'd left it to run into the station after her.

'I don't understand. How did you know I was here?' she asked as they drove away.

'My secretary got in touch with me through the radio phone in my boat and I came straight after you.'

'I'm glad you did. So glad,' she sighed, leaning back in her seat, her head against his shoulder. She shuddered, remembering. 'I hope they don't find her. I couldn't go through that again.'

'Reid should never have taken you there. It was no task for a girl.'

They didn't speak much more until they were on his boat and Petra noticed that he was heading away from Venice. 'Where are we going?'

'To Torcello. You remember we didn't have time to go there when I took you to the other islands.'

Petra didn't feel like going there now; sightseeing was the last thing she felt in the mood for, but she felt too low and depressed to say anything. As Carlo pulled in to the jetty, a man rushed up and took his mooring rope, talking excitedly to him in Italian and gesturing inland. There was an odd gleam in Carlo's eyes as he took her arm and helped her ashore. 'There's someone I'd like you to meet.'

'Now? Oh but Carlo . . .'

But he was walking her quickly along to what looked like a ruin that was in the process of being restored. Nearby there was a line of tents, presumably belonging to the couple of dozen people who were helping with the restoration work. Petra saw a young man with short fair hair who looked vaguely familiar, but then Carlo's grip tightened on her arm and he said, 'Look.'

She turned to see a blonde-haired girl running towards them and stood still, too stunned to move. But then she gave a great shout of 'Sara,' and ran to meet the friend she'd looked for for so long.

Things were pretty emotional for a while and it was some time before they all sat down on the grass in a secluded spot and Petra could think rationally enough to demand an explanation. 'But what are you *doing* here? How did you get here?'

Sara laughed. 'You'll have to blame Steve for that,' she said indicating the young man by her side. 'He arrived at the station in Venice while I was waiting for a train to leave. He came to Italy to help with the American part of the Venice in Peril campaign here in Torcello, and he came over to ask me how to get here. And well, we talked and I ended up coming with him. I've been here ever since.'

'But why didn't you let me know? I've been searching and searching . . .'

'But I did,' Sara interrupted. 'Okay, maybe I did leave it longer than I should have done, but there aren't any public phones on Torcello so I had to wait until we

went into Venice. Then I phoned you in Paris but
Madame Charron said you'd gone back to England. So
I wrote to you there, several times, but I didn't get a
reply. I was beginning to worry about *you*.'

'Oh no. You mean your letters are just sitting on the
doormat at home? I never thought of that,' Petra
groaned.

'And I sent someone to check the flat in Paris but the
woman there merely said that you weren't there, she
never said that you'd phoned again,' Carlo put in.

'Probably because I spoke to old Madame Charron,'
Sara explained. She looked at Carlo. 'That man who
found me; he said that you were the person that rotter
Enrico impersonated. It was your palazzo he took me to.'

'Oh, I'm sorry,' Petra apologised. 'This is Count
Carlo Berini. Carlo, I'd like you to meet my friend Sara
Hamling. At long, long last,' she added with a smile
that was close to tears.

Carlo reached out to cover her hand, a gesture that
wasn't lost on Sara who looked at them both
contemplatively. 'And this is Steve Tracey. His father's
in real estate.'

Petra almost laughed aloud, but she knew her friend
pretty well and knew that she would never have spent
weeks in a tent of all places with someone unless there
was something really special between them.

'But I still don't understand how Carlo finally found
you?' she complained.

'It was through the men at the station who'd been on
holiday; one of them clearly remembered seeing Sara
talking to a young man with a U.S. flag on his luggage.
After that it was easy. Most of the young Americans
who come to Venice spend time in Torcello or at least
visit it. But I didn't have time to make quite certain that
Sara was actually on the island before I got the message

about Reid taking you off to look at that body and had to go after you.'

'Who's Reid?' Sara demanded. 'And what body?'

'I'll tell you some other time,' Petra replied. 'But it really doesn't matter any more.'

They stayed at Torcello all that afternoon and the two girls had a few minutes alone before they left. 'Will you go back to England now?' Sara asked.

'Yes, soon I expect.'

'Why don't you stay here with us? It's fun.'

'No, I don't think so, but I'll come and say goodbye to you before I leave Venice.' Petra added, 'You're serious about Steve, aren't you?'

'Yes, we're going back to America together so that I can meet his family.'

'I hope it works out.'

'I know it will,' Sara said confidently. 'And I really mean it this time,' she added with a laugh. 'I was always saying that, wasn't I?' She paused. 'I hope it works out for you, too, with Carlo. You're in love with him, aren't you? Anyone can see that.'

'Oh dear, I didn't think it showed.'

Sara gave her a quick hug. 'Thanks for looking for me. I'm sorry you had to go through so much worry.'

They waved goodbye to each other as Carlo steered the boat away from the island, waved until they were out of sight. Then Petra put a hand on Carlo's arm. 'Thank you for finding her,' she said simply. 'I'll never be able to repay you for that.'

He covered her hand with his and grinned. 'Oh, I'm sure we'll be able to find a way,' he said wickedly.

Impossible not to know what he meant. Petra flushed and took her hand away, looking ahead towards Venice. 'Now that we've found Sara I'll be able to go back to England,' she said as casually as she could manage.

Carlo glanced at her averted profile and said, 'Oh, I don't think that's a very good idea.'

'You—you don't?'

'No, I think you should go to the Bahamas.'

Petra turned to look at him in astonishment. 'To the Bahamas? To my parents, you mean?'

'Yes. I think we should fly out and meet them next week.'

'We?' Her breath caught in her throat, 'Carlo—just what are you saying?'

'I'm saying that I want to marry you, of course.' He slowed the boat down and turned it into St Mark's Basin towards the Grand Canal.

'But why? Why do you want to marry me, Carlo?'

He looked at her in astonishment. 'You know full well why. Because I'm head over heels in love with you, of course.'

'But I *don't* know.' Silly tears of happiness came to her eyes. 'You've never told me. Not once.'

'Yes, I have, dozens of times.' He hastily turned back to steer the boat under the Academy bridge and up the Canal towards the palazzo. 'Every time we've made love I've told you how much I love you.'

'You idiot!' Petra was so mad she punched him in the ribs. 'How was I to know? When we get to that stage you always switch to Italian.'

'Do I?' He looked surprised, then threw back his head and laughed. 'I'd better tell you now then.' And turning off the engine he pulled her to him. 'I love you, *cara*. I'm crazily, madly, hopelessly in love with you. And if you won't marry me I shall spend my life trying to make you change your mind. Darling Petra, *cara mia. Ho tanto bisogno di te.*'

'You're doing it again,' Petra wailed. 'And what about the boat?' as an angry hooter sounded behind them.

But Carlo pulled her into his arms to show her in a universal language just how he felt, and did it so thoroughly that they created the biggest traffic jam the Grand Canal had known in years.

ROMANCE

Variety is the spice of romance

Each month, Mills & Boon publish new romances. New stories about people falling in love. A world of variety in romance — from the best writers in the romantic world. Choose from these titles in October.

AN IRRESISTIBLE FORCE Ann Charlton
DARK DREAM Daphne Clair
PROMISE OF THE UNICORN Sara Craven
DAUGHTER OF THE SEA Emma Goldrick
FIRE WITH FIRE Penny Jordan
THE BRIDE SAID NO Charlotte Lamb
THE HAWK OF VENICE Sally Wentworth
A STRANGER'S TOUCH Sophie Weston
WILD JASMINE Yvonne Whittal
FUSION Rowan Kirby
*__THAI TRIANGLE__ Jayne Bauling
*__THE ARROGANT LOVER__ Flora Kidd

On sale where you buy paperbacks. If you require further information or have any difficulty obtaining them, write to: Mills & Boon Reader Service, PO Box 236, Thornton Road, Croydon, Surrey CR9 3RU, England.

*These two titles are available *only* from Mills & Boon Reader Service.

Mills & Boon the rose of romance

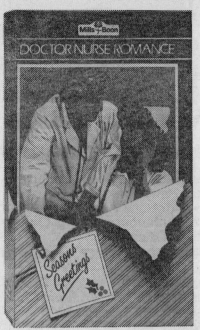

Just what the doctor ordered

The Doctor's Villa
JENNY ASHE

Doctor Knows Best
ANN JENNINGS

Surgeon in the Snow
LYDIA BALMAIN

Suzanne and the Doctor
RHONA TREZISE

Four brand new Doctor/Nurse romances from Mills and Boon, in an attractive Christmas Gift Pack.

Available from 11th October, at £3.99 it's just what the doctor ordered.

The Rose of Romance

Mills & Boon

Take 4
Exciting Books
Absolutely
FREE

Love, romance, intrigue... all are captured for you by
Mills & Boon's top-selling authors. By becoming a
regular reader of Mills & Boon's Romances you can
enjoy 6 superb new titles every month plus a whole
range of special benefits: your very own personal
membership card, a free monthly newsletter packed
with recipes, competitions, exclusive book offers and
a monthly guide to the stars, plus extra bargain offers
and big cash savings.

**AND an Introductory FREE GIFT for YOU.
Turn over the page for details.**

As a special introduction we will send you four exciting Mills & Boon Romances Free and without obligation when you complete and return this coupon.

At the same time we will reserve a subscription to Mills & Boon Reader Service for you. Every month, you will receive 6 of the very latest novels by leading Romantic Fiction authors, delivered direct to your door. You don't pay extra for delivery — postage and packing is always completely Free. There is no obligation or commitment — you can cancel your subscription at any time.

You have nothing to lose and a whole world of romance to gain.

Just fill in and post the coupon today to **MILLS & BOON READER SERVICE, FREEPOST, P.O. BOX 236, CROYDON, SURREY CR9 9EL.**

Please Note:- **READERS IN SOUTH AFRICA** write to **Mills & Boon, Postbag X3010, Randburg 2125, S. Africa.**

FREE BOOKS CERTIFICATE

To: **Mills & Boon Reader Service, FREEPOST, P.O. Box 236, Croydon, Surrey CR9 9EL.**

Please send me, free and without obligation, four Mills & Boon Romances, and reserve a Reader Service Subscription for me. If I decide to subscribe I shall, from the beginning of the month following my free parcel of books, receive six new books each month for £6.60, post and packing free. If I decide not to subscribe, I shall write to you within 10 days. The free books are mine to keep in any case. I understand that I may cancel my subscription at any time simply by writing to you. I am over 18 years of age.

Please write in BLOCK CAPITALS.

Signature _____

Name _____

Address _____

_____ Post code _____

SEND NO MONEY — TAKE NO RISKS.

Please don't forget to include your Postcode.

Remember, postcodes speed delivery. Offer applies in UK only and is not valid to present subscribers. Mills & Boon reserve the right to exercise discretion in granting membership. If price changes are necessary you will be notified.

EP86

6R   Offer expires 31st December 1985